'You said you'd reached a decision.' A lift of Cleo's silky eyebrow gave emphasis to her question. 'May I know what it is?'

'Of course you may,' Jude replied.

So smooth, so suave, so damnably cool. She could have hit him! She couldn't imagine now why she had ever thought she liked him, believed that an expedient marriage to a man such as him would be no intolerable thing.

He lit a slim cigar, taking his time, and the flame of his lighter threw his features into harsh relief. And his eyes, darkened to midnight, dealt her a glancing blow. He'd looked at her before, but never like that, never as if he owned her.

'I have decided,' he regarded the glowing tip of his cigar with lazy interest, 'to agree to your suggestion of an alliance—a marriage of convenience. Successful marriages have been based on less,' he told her. A smile flickered briefly over the long, masculine mouth. 'That is to say, I agree in principle—however, there would be one stipulation. It would have to be a full marriage. I want children!'

*Books you will enjoy
by DIANA HAMILTON*

PAINTED LADY

Reunited with her grandfather at last, Ziggy was beginning to revise her opinion of him and the family feud that had kept them apart for so long. But she wasn't going to change her opinion of Rafe d'Anjou. Wasn't it obvious that his 'interest' in her was purely a selfish one?

THE WILD SIDE

Hannah should have been going on holiday, but instead she found herself kidnapped in a snowbound Norfolk cottage with a contemptuous stranger. At least, Waldo Ross was a stranger to her—but he knew who Hannah was...

A SECURE MARRIAGE

BY

DIANA HAMILTON

MILLS & BOON LIMITED
ETON HOUSE   18-24 PARADISE ROAD
RICHMOND   SURREY   TW9 1SR

All the characters in this book have no existence outside the imagination of the Author, and have no relation whatsoever to anyone bearing the same name or names. They are not even distantly inspired by any individual known or unknown to the Author, and all the incidents are pure invention.

All Rights Reserved. The text of this publication or any part thereof may not be reproduced or transmitted in any form or by any means, electronic or mechanical, including photocopying, recording, storage in an information retrieval system, or otherwise, without the written permission of the publisher.

This book is sold subject to the condition that it shall not, by way of trade or otherwise, be lent, resold, hired out or otherwise circulated without the prior consent of the publisher in any form of binding or cover other than that in which it is published and without a similar condition including this condition being imposed on the subsequent purchaser.

First published in Great Britain 1989 by Mills & Boon Limited

© Diana Hamilton 1989

*Australian copyright 1989
Philippine copyright 1989
This edition 1989*

ISBN 0 263 76248 3

*Set in Times Roman 10 on 11½ pt.
01-8903-58216 C*

Made and printed in Great Britain

CHAPTER ONE

JUDE MESCAL walked through the office and Cleo thought, as she had thought so many times before: he moves like a cat, a mean, moody, magnificent cat.

She had heard other adjectives ascribed to the chief executive of Mescal Slade—cold, remote, terrifying. But one of the many advantages of being the personal assistant to the most powerful man in one of the City's most prestigious merchant banks was a certain degree of invulnerability. Jude Mescal didn't frighten her; nannies were rarely afraid of their charges, they knew them too well. And that was how Cleo sometimes regarded him—as a difficult but gifted charge.

He appeared to be in one of his thankfully rare irascible moods this morning, she decided with a serene half-smile as she noted the way his secretary, Dawn Goodall, cringed at her desk. The way the sedate middle-aged woman was lowering her head, hunching her shoulders and trying to look invisible made Cleo forget her own problems just for a moment.

Jude paused at the heavy, highly polished door to that inner sanctum, his office. He had failed to issue his customary cool good mornings, and the black bar produced by the frowning clench of brows that thundered down above the almost startling azure of his eyes and the forceful line of his nose attested to his ill temper even before the words, 'I'm seeing no one today, Cleo. Cancel all appointments. Understood?' were barked out in that husky, slightly gravelly voice that had the power to make even the chairman of the board look as though he felt like a five-year-old on his first day at school.

'Certainly, Mr Mescal.' Cleo dipped her smooth silver-blonde head, feeling the expertly cut wings of her hair brush against the perfect ivory of her pointed face, hiding the amused smile that hovered around the full, curved contours of her mouth. It was obviously going to be one of those days.

'And bring in the Research file on Chemical Holdings.' He slewed round quickly on the balls of his feet, the blue steel of his eyes turning Dawn Goodall to stone at her desk. 'And if anyone from First Union calls, I'm unavailable until the lunch appointment we arranged for tomorrow. Got that, Mrs Goodall?'

An agonised squawk was the nearest Dawn could get to an acknowledgement, but Cleo chimed in, ultra-sweet and smooth as silk, 'As rumour has it, First Union have been shopping around. Could tomorrow's lunch be the preliminary to a hostile bid?'

She hadn't been able to resist that dig, and for a moment the muscles of his wide shoulders tensed beneath the dark silk and mohair suiting, then his mouth quirked acidly. 'No one makes a bid, hostile or otherwise, for an efficient house. And Mescal Slade's one of the top rankers. Your job is safe, Miss Slade. For the moment. Bring that file through.'

In the silence following the thud as heavy mahogany closed on its frame Dawn let out a pent-up breath,

'The file's right here. I had it brought up from Research first thing. And rather you than me. I'd ask for a transfer to washroom attendant if I didn't need the money I get sitting here.' She scowled at a typing error and Cleo picked up the file, shaking her head,

'You're a damn good secretary, otherwise you wouldn't *be* sitting there,' she told the older woman.

'You've only been working for him for three months, you'll soon learn to ignore the iceberg image. He's a sweetie underneath.'

'If you say so.' Dawn didn't look convinced and Cleo turned away, going into her own small office to collect her notebook, the file from the Equity and Research department tucked under her arm.

Jude Mescal had a reputation for being an iceberg, a well-oiled automaton plugged into his work; remote as a god on top of Olympus, occasionally breathing fire and thunder down on the heads of lesser beings, but not often enough for it to become cause for justifiable complaint.

When she had been appointed as his personal assistant a year ago, with her degree in economics safely in her pocket and her inbred fascination with the world of merchant banking, she had known she could handle the Frozen Asset—as Jude Mescal was popularly and irreverently known. She had countered cool cynicism with a disregard that was in no way negated by her slightly amused smile, met his rare temper outbursts with total equanimity, did her job faultlessly and enjoyed the keen working of his incisive brain, even, latterly, anticipating the way his mind would jump. They made a good team and she was, quite possibly, the only one of Mescal Slade's employees who wasn't openly or secretly afraid of him.

He was standing at one of the windows, looking out, when she walked through. An undeniably attractive hunk, she thought inconsequentially as the cool, smoky grey of her eyes appraised the breadth of shoulder and back, the supple leanness of hip and length of leg. Wealthy, worldly, with a brain as quick and sharp as a rapier, he was one of the City's most eligible bachelors, never without a beautiful woman at his side when the occasion demanded such a decoration, and never—Cleo had noted with wry humour and a somewhat incomprehensible feeling of satisfaction—looking other than politely bored by the adoring postures and antics of the woman in question.

Rumour had it that Jude Mescal was wary, saw all women as mercenary gold-diggers, that he merely used them before they could use him. Idly, she wondered what it would feel like to be dated socially by Jude. Sheer hell, she decided, if boredom was the only emotion that looked out of those remarkable eyes. But if those eyes were to warm into sexual awareness, to intimacy...

'Sit down, Miss Slade.' The command was abrupt and he didn't turn. So Cleo sat, taking the chair angled across the huge leather-topped desk, smoothing the silver grey fabric of her designer suit over her knees. There it was again, 'Miss Slade' for the second time this morning. Annoyed by her dig about the prospect of a hostile takeover bid from the American bankers, First Union? Possibly. Cleo sucked in her breath. So the biter didn't relish the prospect of being bitten!

As if the intensity of her gaze had penetrated his mood of absorption at last, he turned, his eyes briefly flicking over her, moving from the top of her groomed silver-blonde head to the tips of her expensively shod toes.

'Right. To work. Let's see if the findings from Research coincide with my gut reaction about CH.'

He kept her hard at it for over an hour, probing for her reaction to the report, the complicated balance sheets spread out before them, until Dawn came through with the coffee-tray, putting it down on the desk and sidling out apprehensively when Jude eyed the offering as if it were an intrusion of an unspeakably vulgar kind. Although Cleo had tried to reassure the older woman, Dawn didn't appreciate that when he was engrossed in his work he was on another plane entirely; it was nothing personal.

And Cleo, pouring from the chased silver pot, said, 'It stinks,' not meaning the coffee, of course. 'I wouldn't advise a cat to buy into that little lot, let alone our valued Trade Union clients. Can't think why they showed interest in the first place.'

Jude grinned, his whole body appearing to relax as he took the cup she gave him, stirring the brew reflectively although he took neither sugar nor cream.

'Absolutely right.' He looked pleased with her, almost as if he were about to pat her on the head, as if he had been testing her in some way, finding out if her judgement of market trends was sound.

He needn't have gone to the trouble, she thought, her cool, liquid eyes betraying not the slightest hint of her inner amusement as she sipped her coffee. The idea of a literal pat on the head was funny enough in itself; Jude Mescal never descended to personal levels. He was too remote, too cool. And she made it her business to know her chosen profession backwards and inside out. She wasn't big-headed about it, it was simply in her, bred in the bone, so the idea that he might have been testing her had to be amusing. He shouldn't need to be told that a Slade, as well as a Mescal, had banking in the blood.

Although he now seemed marginally more relaxed, the bite was back in the deep husky voice as, his coffee-cup empty and the offer of a refill waved aside, he asked, 'How is John Slade?'

The question didn't surprise her too much; there had been close business connections for decades between the Slades and the Mescals. Since her parents' deaths ten years ago her Uncle John had run the largely family-owned finance house, Slade Securities, until a couple of years ago when he had been forced to retire after a near-fatal heart-attack.

'Not too good,' she replied sadly. Her uncle had become her guardian after the deaths of her parents, the only person to offer her any comfort at all during those earlier, lonely years. 'He has to take things very quietly. We've been warned he mustn't get excited or upset.'

'And your cousin Luke?' Jude's eyes, over steepled fingers, were cool, astute.

Cleo hunched one shoulder, 'Coping in his father's stead, as far as I know. Keeping his nose clean, I hope.'

It was fairly common knowledge that a spiteful piece in a gossip column concerning a brawl Luke had been involved in at some notorious West End nightclub had been responsible for his father's latest and most serious attack, and Cleo could sense the condemnation in Jude's eyes. Luke was brilliant in his way, but emotionally immature, and his father wasn't the only person who thought it was high time he faced up to the responsibilities he now carried. Running a successful finance house demanded more than a clever mind and financial bravado.

Thankfully, Jude let the subject drop, instructing, 'Have a word with Chef. I want tomorrow's lunch arrangements to be perfect. Nothing ostentatious, just the best. You know the drill. And have everything you can lay your hands on pertaining to First Union on my desk in half an hour. And make sure I'm not disturbed. Oh—and Cleo——' this as she was already on her way, file and notepad neatly gathered, thinking with a touch of satisfaction that he *did* have the jitters about the Americans 'have lunch with me. One-thirty?'

Her heart dropped to the soles of her feet and squirmed back up again because the mention of lunch, today, gave her a very sick feeling indeed. But her answering smile was tinged with polite regret, exactly right, as she told him, 'I'm sorry, Mr Mescal. But I've a prior appointment. I would break it if I could, but it's not possible.'

If he was disappointed, he didn't show it. But she was. If she had been free to lunch with him it would have meant that she didn't have that prior date with Robert Fenton.

Robert was the last man she wanted to see, but his telephoned invitation—more of a command, really—late last night had been dark with a threat she didn't want to speculate about too deeply. Not until all the cards were down. She couldn't understand why he wanted to see her and, knowing him, she had been worrying about it all morning. They had parted far from amicably, so why was he insisting they met?

She signed the routine letters and memos Dawn had left on her desk, made a couple of brief inter-office phone calls regarding the details of First Union which were to be sent up, pronto, then took the lift to the executive dining-suite, the back of her mind ticking over the list of precise instructions for Chef, the front of it occupied with regret over the missed opportunity to have lunch with Jude.

They lunched together fairly frequently, sometimes dined at his home in Belgravia, and she always enjoyed the occasions. He used them to put his mind in neutral, allowing it to digest some problem or other, a decision that had to be quickly and correctly reached—no margin for error. She used them to get to know him better, an exercise she found increasingly fascinating. It was essential, she told herself, to know what made one's boss tick. And during those quiet interludes she had gained a rare and, she firmly believed, unique insight, catching glimpses of his droll sense of humour, the underlying deep humanity of the man. And she found that liking for the man himself had been added to respect for his remarkable brain.

Latterly—although there was nothing personal in it, she always assured herself—she had found herself wondering why, at the age of thirty-six, he had never married, never come close to it as far as subtle probings had allowed her to gather. Because, subtle as they were, the steel shutters had always come down decisively whenever he had sensed he was in any danger at all of giving away more of himself than he intended to do.

And Cleo pushed through the swing door into the immaculate kitchens, feeling fraught because she knew full well that lunch with Robert Fenton would be no pleasure at all.

The restaurant Robert had suggested they use was pricey, exclusive and secluded, and she looked at him across the beige linen-covered table and wondered what she had ever seen in him.

At twenty-seven, three years her senior, he was superficially good-looking. His mid-brown hair was a little overlong but superbly cut, his clothes of good quality but a little on the flamboyant side. Compared with Jude Mescal he was a shadow, lacking the other man's strength and sheer presence. Cleo wondered why such a comparison should have come to her mind, and unwillingly remembered how when her cousin Luke had introduced her to Robert Fenton at a party two years ago she had thought he was the cat's whiskers.

Coming to the end of her final year at the LSE she had had little time for dates. But what time she'd had had been spent with Robert, his seemingly effortless charm helping her to relax.

With her Finals behind her at last and her sights fixed on joining Mescal Slade in whatever capacity offered, she had seen more of Robert. Until, her brief infatuation dying an inevitable death on her emergence from those long years of dedicated hard slog, she had at last begun to realise that Robert Fenton was not quite what he seemed. The image he chose to project was at variance with the man inside the skin. And with her eyes wide open at last she had discovered that she rather despised him.

Nothing was said until their order had been taken and then he told her, his hazel eyes sly, 'You're looking more beautiful than ever, Cleo, my love. Work obviously agrees with you. I must try it some time.'

Cleo didn't deign to reply; she was in no mood for facile flattery and she was no longer amused by the way Robert seemed able to afford the best things in life, even though he had no visible means of support. She was no longer the naïve, emotionally backward student who rarely lifted her nose from her books for long enough to look around and find out what people were like.

'Why was it so vitally important that we meet?' she demanded, echoing the words he had uttered over the phone last night, the tone he had used very different from her own cool, almost disinterested one.

He leaned back in his chair, looking at her with lazy eyes.

'You haven't acquired any finesse since I saw you last—when was it? About ten months ago?'

She ignored that. She hadn't needed finesse to tell him to go and take a running jump. And yes, it would have been about ten months ago. She had been Jude's PA for just over two months, still hardly able to believe her good fortune in hearing through the grapevine that the chief executive's then personal assistant would be leaving to have the baby she and her husband had been longing for. That she had landed the job out of a formidable list of applicants had still been responsible for the warm glow of achievement that had totally negated the blow of discovering exactly how perfidious Robert Fenton was. Not that she had still imagined herself in love with him at that time; she had simply been annoyed by her own lack of judgement.

Cleo drank a little of her dry martini, smiled as a waiter placed her order of smoked prawns in front of her, then raised an impatient eyebrow in Fenton's direction. She was in no mood for games.

'It's brass tacks time, is it?' He read her mood. 'I need money, my love. Rather a large amount of the stuff. And you are going to have to divvi up.'

She might have known! His primary interest in her, she had discovered, had always been financial. But the wealthy were always prey to the avarice of others—Aunt Grace had drilled that into her often enough!

'Like hell I am! And if that's all you wanted to say to me, I'm leaving,' she said softly, a distant smile hovering around her mouth because she wasn't worried, not then. She reached for her bag, not willing to waste one more second on this importuning louse.

But he caught her wrist across the table, his fingers hurting. To force him to release her would cause the type of public scene she abhorred, so she subsided, fury tightening her mouth.

'Very wise.' Fenton's voice was suave as he gradually released his hold on her. 'Eat your nice prawns, duckie—this might take some time. You see, it concerns that pillar of respectable society, your good Uncle John. Though he's not so good, healthwise, I hear.'

He tossed back his whisky and soda and clicked his fingers at the hovering wine-waiter. Cleo felt ill, and she was worried now, but there was no emotion in her voice as she interrupted his conversation with the waiter.

'There's no way my uncle can be any concern of yours.'

'No?' He tipped his head as he finished ordering. 'But I am concerned. And he will be concerned about you—about the state of your morals, in particular. Such a highly moral man, your guardian, I hear. And your Aunt Grace is also a pious lady, very concerned with the family image, with some justification. A twenty-room mansion in Herts and a bank account that must be touching the two million mark is an image even I would try to live up to.'

'Will you get to the point?' Cleo snapped, thrown off balance, thrusting aside her untouched starter as her main course of sole appeared.

'The point? Ah—yes.' He cut into his veal, smiling. 'Adverse reports on your morals would not faze Aunt Grace. Annoy her, of course, but it would be something she could handle—especially if the dirt could be swept under the Aubusson. But dear old Uncle John—now there's an entirely different ball game. Two massive heart-attacks already——' He shook his head in a parody of sorrow. 'If he heard what I could tell him—through the gutter press—then the shock could very well finish the old boy off. Especially when we consider that the second attack followed right on the heels of that naughty little piece about his son Luke which appeared in the Dezzi Phipps column. And we wouldn't want that, would we, my love?'

She wanted to hit him. Sitting at the same table with him made her insides heave. His tactics were blackmail, but he had no leverage, and that puzzled her even more than it worried her.

But that state of affairs didn't last long after she hissed, her eyes darkening with disgust, 'You're spouting hot air and garbage! You can have nothing to say about my morals, either way. We dated a few times——'

'Rather more than a few.' The look he gave her made her skin crawl. 'And I think my version of the events that led to our break-up might make more titillating hearing than yours. I'd put it about like so: a poor but honest young man—me——' he dipped his head as she snorted violently, 'falling in love with a beautiful young student. You. A touch promiscuous, but our hero overlooked that—being head over heels, you understand. And then the problems—beautiful student had such expensive tastes, having been brought up in the lap of luxury. This forces our hero to take risks with the small amount he does have—it being common knowledge that no one gets to first base with the lady without vast expenditure. But she has promised to marry him, so he believes the risks he's taking worth it. So he gets deeper into debt: gambling, loan sharks, you name it. All to keep the lady happy. He has to give her a good time because if he doesn't she will find someone who will.'

Cleo's eyes narrowed and she sucked in a deep breath. The man was a lunatic. 'If anyone who knew me, least of all Uncle John, would believe that trash, they'd believe day was night.' She had listened to enough verbal slime to sever her connection with her inbred cool caution, but he quelled the imminent storm with five well chosen words.

'The Red Lion Hotel, Goldingstan.'

Then he relaxed back in his chair, his meal finished, raising an eyebrow at the congealing, untouched food on her plate.

'Not hungry? Pity. However, my dislike of waste is tempered by the knowledge that you are going to pay the bill. You can afford it. I can't. Now, where were we?'

'You were trying to blackmail me,' she clipped, her voice controlled. But she was shaking inside and there was no way she could disguise the disgust on her face, the loathing in her huge dark eyes. 'You make me sick!'

'Now that *is* sad.' His voice was heavy with sarcasm and the smile that curved his lips as he refilled his wineglass made her shudder. 'But I think I'm going to be able to live with that, especially as you are going to settle my debts and get a couple of rather threatening heavies off my back. Oh, and by the way,' his voice was almost a purr as she opened her mouth to categorically deny her intention of doing any such thing, 'I kept the hotel receipt. Mr and Mrs Robert Fenton, room four, on the night of the eleventh of June last year. And in case there's any doubt, I'm sure Mrs Galway—you remember her— the hotelier's wife who was so obliging and told us she never forgot a guest, will be able and willing to identify you as the said Mrs Robert Fenton. She might even be able to recall that we couldn't drag ourselves out of that room until half-eleven the following morning!'

Still smiling his odious smile, he lit a cigarette and blew a cloud of smoke across the table. 'Not that it will come to asking Mrs Galway to identify you. You've no intention of being awkward about this, have you, my love?'

'Don't call me that!' she rasped, her voice hoarse, as though her throat had turned to sandpaper. She was more disgusted by his repeated use of the endearment than anything else. It was a crazy reaction, but that was the way it was, and she wanted to get away from him, get the whole distasteful episode over, so she asked stonily, 'How much?'

'Twenty-five thousand.'

She didn't believe it at first. But she saw from his face that he was serious, deadly serious, and she laughed, without humour.

'You're mad! Where would I get that kind of money? And even if I could, do you honestly think I'd believe keeping the Red Lion incident secret worth that amount?'

Leaning forward across the table he called her bluff,

'I think you'd consider it worth it at twice the price. Can you imagine dear old John's face if he read a headline that might go something like: *"Slade Securities Chief's Niece Involved in Debt Scandal"* With an opening paragraph that could say something like: *"Slade heiress's lover threatened with knee-capping by loan shark's heavy mob. 'I'm in real trouble. I only got in debt for her sake,' explained Robert Fenton, Cleo Slade's former lover. 'She's used to the best and she said she loved me. But she won't lift a finger to help now I'm in this mess. I'm devastated,' added the distraught Mr Fenton."* Or something similar.' He stubbed his cigarette out and Cleo felt the trap close more tightly around her, squeezing until she thought she would die of it.

Yes, she could just imagine what that kind of publicity could do to Uncle John—the piece about Luke had been mild in comparison and that, as almost everyone believed, had brought on that second, near fatal heart-attack. And it wouldn't exactly ease her career along, either, but that was a minor consideration beside the damage it could do to her uncle.

Fenton added, 'What's a mere twenty-five thousand to a girl who will inherit her father's share of the Slade Millions in—what will it be? Around a year's time? A drop in the proverbial ocean!'

Her mouth tightened. 'Can the heavy mob—in which, incidentally, I don't believe—wait a year? I don't inherit until I'm twenty-five, as you very well know.'

'Or until you marry,' he put in slyly. 'I did my homework.'

'And are you going to suggest I marry you to get my hands on the money?' She wouldn't put it past him, and there was an edge of hysteria in her voice and it sharpened his eyes.

'I'm not that stupid. Should you marry before you reach your twenty-fifth birthday, then, in order to obtain an early release of your considerable inheritance, your guardians, your so upright and proper uncle and aunt, would have to unreservedly approve your choice of husband. And they wouldn't have to dig very deep to realise that no way could they approve of yours truly. No,' he smiled oilily, 'I've always known that wasn't on the cards, although at one time I had hopes of keeping you sweet until you were twenty-five and free, not only to inherit, but to marry whomsoever you pleased. But the Fenton charm didn't blind you for long enough. I did ask you to marry me, though, remember? I was beginning to realise you weren't as starry-eyed as you had been, so I suggested we marry and, in true romantic tradition, keep it a secret from those stuffy relatives of yours. I thought that might have set the little female heart pounding away again. However,' he sighed theatrically, 'that wasn't to be, so I've given the matter much thought and decided to cut my losses and settle for twenty-five thou. You can raise it somehow—with your collateral.'

He beckoned for the bill and stood up, pushing the folded slip of paper between the fingers of her clenched hand.

'See you, my love. And thanks for the lunch. I'll keep in touch. Oh, and by the way, I'll want my little pressie in four weeks' time. Cash, if you please.'

Cleo was in her office early the following morning. The thickly carpeted corridors had been silent as she'd walked through the hushed building with the uniformed commissionaire's cheery words echoing hollowly in her head. 'Good morning, Miss Slade. A real touch of spring in the air today!'

The early morning City streets might be awash with warm April sunlight, but winter was in her heart; icy, steel-edged winter.

Her features taut and expressionless, she hung her coat in her cupboard and smoothed the long, narrow lapels of the deep mulberry-coloured Escada suit she was wearing. Expertly applied make-up went some way to hide the pallor induced by a sleepless night and the eyes that met her in the mirror on the back of the cupboard door were sharp with determination.

She had no way of knowing if Robert Fenton was in debt, was being hounded for repayment. It didn't really signify. His threat to her uncle, via herself, was real enough. That kind of heavy blackmail, the threat of the worst kind of publicity in one of the seamier tabloids, would finish the already frail old man. She had no doubt that Fenton could get the slimiest publicity possible. He knew some very dubious characters in the newspaper world, men who didn't care what was printed, or whose lives were shattered, so long as it sold papers.

There was no way she could raise that kind of money without approaching the trustees. And they would, quite rightly, want to know details. And that kind of detail she couldn't give.

She sat at her desk, her spine upright, staring at the polished surface. For the first time ever she regretted the restrictions her father had placed on her massive inheritance.

Throughout her life she had never wanted for material things. Her allowance had been on the generous side, but sensible, and her life with her parents and, later, with her uncle and aunt, had been discreetly luxurious—until, needing to be in London while she was studying, she had persuaded the trustees to buy the small terraced house in Bow where she still lived. She had nothing personal to sell that would raise anything like the amount Fenton was demanding. But unless she was able to raise it, in four weeks' time, Fenton would see those vile lies printed. They had all seen the damage such malicious tittle-tattle had done when Luke's exploits had been snidely publicised and the specialist had warned that the frail old man be treated with kid gloves, that upsets and worry had to be avoided at all costs. So she had to raise that money! She couldn't have his death on her conscience!

Hearing the snick of the outer office door as it opened, she held her breath. It was Jude, as she had hoped, early, well before Dawn was due to arrive. And now had to be the best time to speak to him.

Her breath caught flutteringly in her throat and her stomach wriggled about uncomfortably as she watched him walk past her partly open door to his own office, the inevitable briefcase in his hand. The immaculately cut dark suit he wore clothed his body with easy elegance, and the crisp whiteness of his shirt contrasted sharply with his dark blue tie, with the natural darkness of his skin tones. He always looked as if he had a tan.

Quelling an unwanted spasm of nerves—apprehension had been talked out of her plans during the long, lonely hours of last night, hadn't it?—she rose to her feet and squared her slim shoulders. She had wrestled with the problem Fenton had presented her with and as far as she could see there was only one viable solution— and she had looked long and hard for alternatives. So there was no point in giving way to the jitters now.

The man could always say no. He had said no to business deals before now. But only ever after giving the matter full consideration, after a careful weighing of the pros and cons. He surely wouldn't turn her business proposition down out of hand.

Drawing in a long breath, she tapped lightly on his door and walked in, her features severe, cool, her heart not picking up speed by the smallest fraction. She had learned the trick of unemotionalism in a hard school. She met the vivid azure of his eyes, the small, courteously pleasant smile as he acknowledged her brief greeting. And before he could launch into plans for the day's work, or return his attention to the papers he had already extricated from the black leather briefcase, Cleo dragged a quick breath in through her nostrils and asked, 'Mr Mescal—will you marry me?'

CHAPTER TWO

FOR an agonisingly drawn-out moment Cleo thought he was going to refuse her without giving the matter any consideration at all. His body grew still, very still, before a ghost of a smile flickered briefly around the hard male mouth and was then erased, as if it had never been, as if she had dreamed it.

And then, as he still remained silent, her spine stiffened with impatience beneath the smooth, expensive fabric of her suit. Was he going to say nothing, nothing at all? What if he, like the gentleman he was, ignored her question? What if he treated her startling proposal of marriage as a regrettable mental aberration on her part, deeming it kinder, more polite, to pretend the words had never been said?

Well, in that case, she would just have to repeat her offer, she decided with grim stoicism. Against all her expectations she felt perspiration slick the palms of her hands and, slowly, she ran the tip of her tongue over lips gone suddenly dry. At that, as if her physical unease had recalled him, made some impact on his mind, he gestured her to a chair with an almost imperceptible movement of his hand. And Cleo sat, glad to, because for some reason her knees felt as if they were about to give way.

Silently, her eyes too big for her face, she willed him to answer, to say he'd give it some thought, at least. His agreement was the only solution she could see to a grotesque problem, and she needed it. For her uncle's sake she needed it.

But now, without knowing how or why it should have crept in, there was an indefinable something going on inside her head that warned her that his acquiescence was important on an entirely different plane. Whatever it was, she couldn't understand it, although she felt she should, and, whatever it was, it made her feel light-headed, breathless.

'And?' he said at last, his tone prompting, his eyes holding hers from beneath thick, dark lashes.

Thrown off balance by the softly put question, the probing she hadn't expected, not in that nebulous form, her smoky eyes widened again, filling her face, while a faint flush of colour stole into her pale skin. 'And?' she repeated, parrot-fashion, her mouth dry.

'And why the unexpected interest?' Jude supplied. 'We've worked together for twelve months, very amicably, I do agree, but I've yet to see signs of a deathless passion from you. Neither,' his voice continued, polite in inflexion, perfectly level, 'do you strike me as being the type of woman who would be desperate for the married status—at any price.'

He was wrong there, she was desperate, but not for the reasons he imagined. Marriage, for the sake of it, had never appealed. She had learned how to be sufficient unto herself, not to need emotional props. But marriage to someone as undeniably suitable as Jude Mescal would be in the eyes of her guardians was the only answer to her awful problem.

But now, at least, he was asking her to give logical answers to her own seemingly illogical question, and she could handle that. For a moment back there she had felt herself to be losing her grip on the tangible, admitting the intangible—that nebulous thread—into her mind so that a union with this man had, for a strange, disjointed moment, seemed important on an entirely unexpected level.

And that particular reaction, she told herself firmly, was due to the momentary panic of nerves. She hadn't expected to feel nervous—so nervous, at least.

She began to relax, feeling the tension drain out of the tautly held muscles of her back and neck. She was completely at home with the unequivocal logic of facts, and she was fully prepared to present him with those facts—as far as she deemed entirely necessary.

She clasped her hands loosely together in her lap and her eyes were cool and frank as she told him, 'Under the terms of my father's will I don't come into my inheritance for another year, and I need a rather large amount now. However, if I marry before then, provided my uncle and aunt approve my choice, my father's money automatically passes to me. They would approve of you, and if we married within, say, three weeks, I could control my inheritance, use the money I need. It wouldn't be a great deal,' she assured him, in case he thought she would spend the lot and then expect him to keep her in luxury. 'Not when seen in context. My future inheritance is popularly known as the Slade Millions.'

He dipped his head in brief acknowledgement of the facts that were, after all, common knowledge in City circles, and she knew the facts had been concisely put, the reason for her proposal made clear enough. She was devastated when he chuckled, a rare occurrence indeed for the Frozen Asset!

His incredible azure eyes were irradiated with amusement and Cleo, looking at him, felt her skin crawl with hot colour. To ask him to marry her had been humiliating enough in itself, without him adding to her discomfort by treating the whole thing as a joke!

'Wouldn't it have been simpler to arrange a loan?' The amusement lingered for a while, sparkling in his eyes, then faded, leaving his face as it ever was—remote, cool, intelligent. 'Embarking on the commitment of marriage seems rather drastic. Couldn't you approach the trustees of your late father's estate? Come to that,' his wide shoulders lifted fractionally, 'I could lend you what you need. Your credit rating is excellent,' he added drily.

He sat down then, taking his chair on the opposite side of the huge desk, his clever eyes narrowed over steepled fingers as he watched her. 'How much? And what for?'

But Cleo shook her head decisively, the shimmering silver fall of her hair swinging across her face. 'I'd prefer not to borrow.' She didn't want anyone to know why she needed the money, and anyone prepared to lend that amount would certainly demand to know where the money was going! And her eyes met his in unconscious, mute appeal and he asked her softly, 'Are you in some kind of trouble?'

Again the sharp negating swing of her head; the mess she was in was of her own making, she would extricate herself from it in her own way, without involving anyone else in the sordid details. She had made a mistake, a bad one, when she had allowed herself to be infatuated by Robert Fenton's silver tongue, his easy charm. But she had learned her lesson and was about to pay dearly for it. And sitting here, mutely supplicant under the remote eyes of the man who was known never to suffer involvement—except with his work—suddenly became unbearable.

She should never have dreamed up the idea, and clearly she was getting nowhere. The slow burn of anger started inside her, making her hate herself for the foolishness that had brought her to this totally humiliating position, hate Robert Fenton for the slimy, blackmailing creep he was, hate Jude Mescal for taking her vulnerability and examining it like something curious on the end of a pin.

She started to scramble to her feet, wanting nothing more than to get away from those coolly analytical eyes, but his voice stopped her.

'I can gather, roughly, what you would stand to gain from marriage. But it involves two. So can you tell me what I would get out of a situation I've spent my adult life steering well clear of?'

The slightly sardonic lift of heavy black brows, the look of superiority and distance the gesture imparted to his unforgettably strong features boosted the slow fuse of her anger, creating an explosion that errupted in scalding words.

'Rumour has it that you've never committed yourself to a woman because you're afraid of tying yourself to a gold-digger,' she snapped insultingly. 'If you married me you'd know I hadn't married you for your money. I've more than enough of my own—or will have! And I inherit a sizeable block of Slade Securities shares, which I could be persuaded to turn over to you—and I'd have thought that might interest you more than somewhat! And if that isn't enough——'

'Enough to be going along with,' he interrupted, and she was glad of that, because she'd run out of reasons, and all she had left was hot air and bluster.

The shares had been her best card; if he married her and she gave him her voting rights he would have the majority shareholding, and that, surely, would be tempting to a man such as he.

She held her breath, her heart pumping, sensing she had his interest now, and he commented, rising to his feet, almost smiling,

'May I have time to give your——' he hesitated, but only fractionally '—your delightful offer the consideration it merits?' And, taking the carefully blank expression on her face for acquiescence, he glanced at his watch and returned his attention to the papers strewn on his desk.

'I shall be away over the weekend and in Brussels on Monday. So shall we have dinner on Monday evening?' His eyes drifted over her slender height as she pushed herself to her feet, making her feel uncharacteristically gauche, dry-mouthed and tongue-tied. 'I'll send Thornwood to pick you up at seven-thirty.'

Cleo left her car on the sweep of gravel at the front of Slade House and carried her overnight grip towards the impressive Edwardian building. She rarely visited now, but she needed to see her uncle and aunt, to reassure herself that she was doing the right thing in not allowing herself to follow her instincts and tell Fenton to go ahead and do his worst because she wouldn't give him one of her nail parings!

She hadn't phoned to let them know to expect her; her mind had been edgy, jumpily occupied with trying to work out how Jude's 'considerations' would take him, which way he would jump. She had learned to anticipate the way his mind worked when it came to complicated dealings in his capacity of chief executive of one of the most successful merchant banks in the City. But this was different, very different. And the more she had tried to extend her own mind, to tune it in to his, the more confused and uncertain she had become. She couldn't get him out of her mind.

When the butler opened the door she wiped the frown from her brow, her voice level and cool,

'Good afternoon, Simmons. Is my aunt in?' then walked past him into the huge hall. 'They're not expecting me, I'm afraid.' She surrendered her camel trenchcoat, her cream kid gloves, the overnight grip, and the butler's expressionless mask gave nothing away; not surprise, certainly not pleasure. No one, not even the servants in this huge luxurious house, was spendthrift when it came to displaying emotions, or in having emotions, quite probably.

'Mrs Slade is in the drawing-room, miss. I'll see your things are taken to your room.'

'Thank you, Simmons.' She turned away, her graceful stride taking her over the polished parquet to find her aunt.

Ten years ago she had been fourteen years old, and she had come to this house because her parents had been drowned when their yacht had capsized in a freak storm off the Cornish coast. She had looked, then, for affection, warmth—for mere interest, even—but had found nothing save a cool concern for her material well-being. She had been luxuriously housed, fed the right food, sent to the right schools, but that was as far as the caring had gone. She had never found the warmth of affection she had so desperately craved in those first terrible years of bereavement. And as she had grown older she had learned to do without it.

Only her uncle had ever taken any interest in her. He had seen her as a person, with needs of her own, fears and hopes of her own, rather than just another responsibility. He was fond of her, she knew, in his own abstracted way. But he had been more often in his office than at home and she had seen little of him. And when he had gone into semi-retirement, due to illness, she, of course, had been living and studying in London, visiting rarely.

Grace Slade was in the drawing-room, a tea-tray on a low table beside her. She was a spare, formidably handsome woman and it was a beautiful room, perfect. But then the Slades demanded perfection in everything, even in people. It was hard to live up to such standards.

'This is a surprise.' Her aunt's voice was coloured with asperity, just a tinge of it, and Cleo sighed. She should have phoned, would have done, but her mind had been in a tangle.

She sank down on a Regency sofa which was upholstered in oyster brocade and said, 'I'd like to stay overnight, drive back tomorrow after lunch.' She was stating her right to be here, using cool dignity. This house was her home, her aunt one of her guardians, for another year. Inhibiting, but a fact. And Grace had taught her by example how to stand on her dignity. Yes, her aunt had taught her well. But sometimes Cleo wondered if the sterility of dignity, of the austere self-command she had learned to wear like a cloak, made her lacking as a human being. Wondered if the suppression of deep emotion was a loss, turning her into a machine, programmed to display good manners, breeding and dedication to the duty which was the good standing of the family.

But now, looking at her aunt—poised, elegant, in perfect control—Cleo decided that she had probably chosen the right path when she had sought to please by emulation, all those years ago, when gaining the approval of her aunt, and possibly her affection, had been something she had striven for. And her single foray into the realm of emotion had been a disaster, landing her in her present sordid predicament. It would never happen again.

'Shall I ring for fresh tea?' Grace wanted to know, her eyes dispassionate. 'You look tired after your drive.'

As well she might, Cleo thought drily, but it had nothing to do with the drive. Two sleepless nights in a row, the image of Jude Mescal tormenting her mind, would hardly make her look sparkling. But she said, 'No tea for me, thank you, Aunt. How is Uncle?'

'As well as can be expected. He frets about the business, which doesn't help. As I've repeatedly told him, it's in Luke's hands now.'

They talked for a while, their conversation polite but wary, until Cleo excused herself and went to find her uncle. He was in the library, the most comfortable room in the house in Cleo's opinion, sitting on the leather chesterfield, a photograph album open on his knees.

'The older I get the more I tend to peer into the past,' was his greeting. Cleo wasn't surprised; Uncle John often came out with such statements, seemingly apropos of nothing, it was one of the humanising things about him that had made her fonder of him than she was of either her aunt or her cousin Luke. 'No one told me you were coming.' His mild eyes questioned her and she sat down beside him, sinking into the squashy leather.

'No one knew. I just arrived—it was a spur of the moment decision.'

'Ah.' He looked vaguely puzzled, as if he couldn't comprehend a decision being taken, just like that. Years of living with Aunt Grace had made him very careful, very precise, leaving nothing to chance.

'And how are you?' Her smoky eyes searched his face. He looked older, much more frail than when she'd seen him last a couple of months ago.

'I'm as well as can be expected, so they tell me.' A fleeting look of terror, so brief it almost wasn't there— because the occupants of Slade House didn't betray emotion, even fear of dying—flickered over his gaunt features, and Cleo, understanding, changed the subject.

'Is Luke expected home this weekend?' She hoped not. Her cousin was pompous and stiff, he always had been, even when he'd been seventeen to her fourteen and she'd tried to make friends with the only young person in a household that had seemed to consist of elderly, rigid machines. But he had been pompous even then, stand-offish, making it clear he didn't like her, considered her addition to the household an invasion of privacy. Luke's attitude had been primarily responsible for her decision to seek work elsewhere, rather than join the family firm of Slade Securities.

'No, he's tied up with some meetings. Look——' a finger stabbed at the open album on his knee, as if he found the subject of Luke too difficult to talk about, and Cleo wondered if she'd touched a sore spot, reminding John Slade of the spiteful piece in that gossip column that had pointed out the other side of his son's character—the reckless, belligerent, hidden side. 'That's your father and me. A village cricket match well over fifty years ago. I was sixteen, your father almost eighteen.'

Cleo peered at the faded print; two youths in white flannels, holding bats, looking impossibly solemn. She grinned, recognising the jut of her father's jaw, an early indication of the stubborn, determined character he would develop in later life. And John Slade, mistaking the reason for her amusement, shook his head,

'It's probably impossible for you to imagine us as ever being young men, or children. But we were, my goodness we were! We were both high-spirited, a little arrogant, and we knew where we were going—or thought we did.' His shoulders slumped a little, his eyes looking into the distant past. 'I'm afraid we both left it late to marry, to get a family, your father even later than I—so you young things must think we were born old! But I can assure you, that wasn't the case!'

'You must still miss him,' Cleo probed gently. At times she still keenly felt the loss of both her parents, and perhaps that was something that might draw her closer to her uncle. For the first time in her adult life she felt she needed to be close to someone, and her uncle touched her hand, just briefly, as if such a demonstration of affection embarrassed him. But it was enough, and his fingers still touched the surface of the photograph, as if he could recapture lost days, lost youth, through the sense of touch—as if he were holding on to a past that was precious because it had held promises, promises which had never been truly fulfilled, she now divined with sudden insight.

And then, in that moment, sitting beside the man whose years were all behind him, she knew she couldn't bring the bitterness of family shame to darken his declining years or, maybe and quite possibly, deprive him of those few remaining years.

Her decision to pay Fenton what he demanded had been the right one. And the only way she could gain access to her inheritance straight away was through marriage. So her proposal to Jude had been the only way out.

And then, out of nowhere, the appalled thought came: What *have* I done? She had asked for the Frozen Asset's hand in marriage, that was what she had done! And, the right, the only thing to do, suddenly became terrifying. What his final decision would be, heaven only knew. He'd probably fire her and suggest she spend the next six months in a rest home!

She wanted to give way to the unprecedented feeling of hysteria she could feel building up inside her—to shriek and scream and hurl things around the room to relieve the pressure inside her head. Instead, she asked her uncle if he'd like her to go with him for a short walk in the garden—the weather was remarkably good for the time of year, wasn't it?

She had been jittery all day, Jude on her mind making her unable to concentrate. She kept thinking of the enormity of what she had done in asking him to marry her, and she wanted to buy a plane ticket to the other side of the world.

She had thought that marriage to such a suitable man would be the answer to her problems. Her intellect had assured her that she would not enter such a business arrangement—which was basically what the marriage would be—empty-handed, far from it, and she was presentable, she wouldn't be a wife he need be ashamed of. And as far as she knew there wasn't a lovely lady in the background—not one he had considered marrying, at least. He was reputedly wary where the state of matrimony was concerned.

There would probably be women for him in the future; she didn't doubt that he possessed his full measure of male sexuality. But provided he was discreet she would be tolerant, understanding. And the hot little pain that made itself felt at the direction her thoughts were taking was solely due to her state of apprehension over the outcome of his 'considerations'—surely it was?

However, what had seemed such a neatly feasible idea began to look like a crass, idiotic blunder. Crasser and more idiotic as the minutes ticked away, their growing total an insupportable weight as Monday morning turned into Monday afternoon...

Unable to bear the suddenly stifling confines of her office a moment longer, she left early, taking the tube back to Bow and entering her own small terraced house, looking for the relief it always gave her.

Her home was her sanctuary, inviolate, the furnishings, the décor, echoing her own cool yet gentle character. It had provided a haven during her years of study and, later, a place to unwind in, to potter around wearing old jeans and shirts after the concentrated mind-stretching that being at Jude Mescal's beck and call all day often entailed.

But this afternoon tranquillity had been forced through the walls as her thoughts, despite all her best efforts, centred on the outcome of her dinner engagement with him later this evening.

Catching sight of herself in the mirror in the hallway, she stopped in her tracks. It was like looking at a crazy woman! Her grey eyes looked haunted, half wild with worry, and far too large for her pale, pointed face.

One look at such a distraught creature, she decided, would be enough to put any man off the idea of marriage—let alone Jude Mescal, who was definitely choosier than most.

And if she were to arrive at his house looking even half-way normal then it was time to take herself firmly in hand, she decided grimly. Deliberately assuming the cloak of self-command, of dignity, that her years with the austere Grace Slade had taught her to wear with ease, she ran a bath, pouring in expensive essence, then relaxed in the perfumed water, planning what she would wear, wondering if she could make time to give herself a facial. She didn't look further ahead than that. She dared not—not if she was to remain in control of herself.

At seven-thirty precisely she was stepping into the Rolls, her voice light and pleasant as she replied to a remark Thornwood had made about the mildness of the weather.

Thornwood was a dear, one of a dying breed, Jude often said. Cleo had met him and his wife, Meg, on several occasions and had marvelled at how well they ran Jude's house between them. They made it a home.

As the luxurious car whispered through the streets towards the quiet square in Belgravia where Jude lived, Cleo took stock. The discipline she had at last been able to bring to her preparations for this evening had transformed her from near nervous wreck into a composed, sophisticated young woman—the sort who would never get the jitters over anything—the sort of creature she had been until she had decided to propose to Jude Mescal, she admitted with a wry half-smile.

He could only say no, and if he did she would have to think of some other way out of the mess she was in. And if he did say no, it wouldn't be because she looked like a crazy woman!

Her black silk dress, falling in wide pleats from a high square yoke and supported by two narrow ribbon straps, was vaguely twenties in style, rather expensive, and the perfect foil for her slender height, for the pale silver gilt of her hair which hung in a shimmering, newly washed curve to her jawline.

No, her image wouldn't let her down tonight, and as long as she could control her nerves—and her temper if he should turn scathing or flippant—then she would be able to manage perfectly. That he might actually agree to marry her, and solve the problem of Fenton, was something she thought it wiser not to consider just now. It was, on the whole, rather too much to hope for, and if she didn't allow herself to hope then she wouldn't be too disappointed when he replied in the negative, as any right-minded man would do.

Even thinking along those lines brought a sudden return of the hated stomach-churning apprehension—to come out of this evening's encounter with her job intact was the most she could hope for—but her inner disturbance wasn't allowed to show as Thornwood held the car door open for her.

She slid the elegant length of her silk-clad legs to the pavement and walked with all her customary grace up the steps towards the panelled front door which Meg already held open in welcome.

CHAPTER THREE

JUDE turned as Meg ushered Cleo into the drawing-room. He held a glass in his hand and had been apparently lost in contemplation of a misty seascape which hung above the Adam fireplace. Strange—the thought brushed Cleo's mind fleetingly—why the intent scrutiny when he must know the painting brush-stroke by brush-stroke? And he had once told her that he didn't much like it but hadn't the heart to throw it out since he had inherited it from his uncle, along with this house.

Her knees shook a little; he looked so improbably handsome in the formal elegance of his dinner-jacket, and now she was looking at him with different eyes. She was accustomed to reacting to him on a business level, regarding him as a much-liked, respected boss, and the way he looked just didn't come into it. But it was coming into it now, and it shouldn't because what she had suggested had, after all, been a business arrangement.

Giving herself a mental shake, she endured the appraising drift of his eyes. His assessment of the way she looked was gentle, like a caress, and she returned his slight smile.

'How was Brussels?'

'Smooth. No problems. There's no danger now of an American takeover, you'll be pleased to know. But you didn't come here to talk about Brussels.'

His smile was tight and gave no impression of warmth and Cleo sank on to a chair and thought, my God! What have I let myself in for? Then she let her eyes laze around the room because it was peaceful, an anodyne for fraying nerve-ends, an harmonious mix of fine antiques, good fabrics, nothing showy. She had been here before on one or two occasions, enjoyed herself. She didn't think she was going to find this evening enjoyable.

He had been pouring the white wine he knew she preferred and she took the glass from him, careful that their fingers should not touch. And one corner of his mouth quirked in a smile, as if he knew just how careful she had been.

Something caught in Cleo's throat; either he was enjoying this, creating a tension calculated to shred the staunchest nerves, or he was waiting for her to make the opening gambit. And she would have done, simply to get it over, behind her, but she didn't know what to say.

Suddenly, the enormity of what she had put in motion when she had proposed to him hit her again, right in the gut. He couldn't have seriously considered her crazy offer—so why was he spinning the agony out? She wished she could shrivel away, become invisible. She didn't know what was happening to her—one minute she was in control, quite calm, the next she was on the verge of hysterics. It wasn't in character for the woman she knew herself to be. And she could stand no more of it!

'Have you reached a decision?' she blurted, her voice thick. She put her glass down on the small round table at the side of her chair, her fingers clumsy, fumbling, and she looked up in time to catch his expression of surprise at her unpolished question and could have bitten her tongue out. Where was the poised image now? she groaned inwardly, resisting the impulse to wring her hands.

But the fleeting look of surprise was gone, his impressive features displaying little more than polite interest as he stood with his back to the crackling wood fire, his whisky glass held loosely in one hand. His eyes were veiled, thrown into shadow so that she couldn't read what was going on inside his head. She probably wouldn't have liked it if she could.

He nodded briefly, 'I have, but we'll talk about it over dinner.' And that told her nothing, nothing at all. If he was trying to test her nerve, her ability to keep cool in the face of mental pressure, he was doing an excellent job!

Lifting her glass again, she recalled how he'd often probed for her reactions to balance sheets, research reports. She had never failed herself on that score—but this probing, if such was his intention, was something else, something more closely allied to emotion than to hard, indisputable fact.

Trouble was, she was unused to handling emotion, and she hadn't, until now, equated it with that proposal of marriage.

So she searched for something to say, something light but not inane, and kept talking, with the occasional interjection from him, until Meg came in with a heated trolley and Cleo realised that the palms of her hands were hot, slippery with sweat, that her insides had turned to jelly with the sheer nerve-shredding effort of trying to look and sound in control of herself.

Meg and her trolley broke the tension, just a little, and Jude said, 'You don't mind if we eat in here?'

She rose fluidly, noting the oblong linen-covered table in the window alcove for the first time.

Long velvet curtains were drawn, closing out the blue April twilight, and candles were lit, creating an atmosphere of intimacy, drawing glittery lights from silver and crystal, casting a softening, warming glow over the cool features of the man opposite, making them enigmatic but not fearsomely so.

The food was delicious, Meg's unobtrusive service effortless. The wine was friendly, relaxing, as was Jude's attitude, his conversation. But Cleo didn't relax, not for a moment, and Meg's superbly cooked food tasted like nothing. However, only when Meg had gone, leaving them with the silver coffee-pot, did she allow a little of all that pent-up anxiety to show through.

'I don't want coffee.' Her voice came out as a snap as his hand hovered over the bone handle of the Queen Anne pot. Then, 'Thanks,' she added, mumbling now. The man was inhuman. Didn't he know how this suspense was pulling her apart?

He hesitated, then poured a cup for himself, and Cleo thought, it's crunch time, and cursed for the fiery colour she felt creeping over her skin.

'Well——' They both started to speak at once and he dipped his head, waving her on, and Cleo wished she'd kept her mouth shut. The onus was on her again, and he knew how to turn the screw.

But enough was enough, she decided savagely, and producing the courage, the composure, from somewhere she remarked levelly, 'You said you'd reached a decision.' A lift of one silky eyebrow gave emphasis to her question. 'May I know what it is?'

'Of course you may.'

So smooth, so suave, so damnably cool. She could have hit him! She couldn't imagine now why she had ever thought she liked him, believed that an expedient marriage to a man such as him would be no intolerable thing.

He lit a slim cigar, taking his time, and the flame of his lighter threw his features into harsh relief, sharpening every slashing angle, every plane. And his eyes, darkened to midnight, dealt her a glancing blow, knocking the breath clear out of her lungs because he'd looked at her before, of course he had, but never like that, never as if he owned her.

'I have decided,' he regarded the glowing tip of his cigar with lazy interest, 'to agree to your suggestion of an alliance—a marriage of convenience. Successful marriages have been based on less,' he told her, his magnificent eyes lifting from their inscrutable contemplation of the glowing tip, meeting the hazy smoke-grey of hers. A smile flickered briefly over the long, masculine mouth. 'That is to say, I agree in principle—however, there would be one stipulation.'

Cleo stared, her eyes wide, hardly able to take it in as the breath she hadn't known she'd been holding was expelled silently from her burning lungs. If Jude Mescal had accepted her proposal of marriage then the idea couldn't have been as demented as she'd come to believe it was. And she need no longer lie awake at nights worrying about the likelihood of failing to pay the money Fenton demanded. She would have control of her inheritance once she was married, and the whole dreadful business could be kept quiet. Everything was going to be all right!

A sudden smile of utter relief made her face radiant, and Jude raised one black eyebrow. 'Don't look so delighted. You haven't heard my stipulation yet.'

'No. No, I haven't.' She felt light-headed. Her conscience wouldn't have to bear the burden of knowing she had been instrumental in darkening her uncle's declining months with shame and misery or, even worse, being the cause of another and almost certainly fatal heart-attack. And Jude's stipulation, whatever it was, couldn't be too daunting.

She tilted her head in easy enquiry, the movement elegant, eloquent, and saw the way his eyes narrowed on her pointed face, on the warm curve of her lips as he said, 'It would have to be a full marriage. I want children.'

The long, square-ended fingers of one hand flexed round the handle of the coffee-pot and, watching them, letting the words he'd said sink in, Cleo felt her insides clench. Fool that she was, she hadn't viewed marriage to him from that angle, merely from the academic side. Two compatible adults merging their lives, their assets, for mutual benefit—that was the way she'd seen it. A marriage of convenience, a business arrangement, made tolerable by their mutual respect.

A full marriage, having children, meant sleeping together, having sex. It put an entirely complexion on the whole idea. Sex without love seemed unconscionably squalid in her view. But not in his, obviously. And why, oh, why hadn't she at least considered the possibility that he might demand a full, physical marriage? Because her head had been too full of the need to take control of her inheritance, she answered herself drily, to think about what Jude Mescal might want!

She stared at the tablecloth, as if the fine fabric held a weird fascination, quite unable to meet his eyes as the beginnings of a slow, deep flush made itself felt. She knew those clever azure eyes were on her, analysing her reaction, and she strove to keep calm.

She had seen the outcome of his acceptance only from her narrow viewpoint, as a means of enabling her to pay off Fenton, shield Uncle John. She had looked no further than that, believing that Jude would view the union as a business arrangement, too, that the offer of the Slade Securities shares and the addition of her own considerable fortune to his might be enough.

However, he was not a eunuch and naturally enough he wanted children, and as a male he was biologically different and could enjoy sex without love; his emotions would not have to be involved. And if he wanted children then it would be her duty, as his wife, to produce them. But could she go through with such a marriage—to a man she did not love?

She would have to, the answer came starkly. She was no twittery, starry-eyed teenager, and if she accepted the benefits of his acquiescence then she must accept the other. The alternative, Fenton's foul threat to go to the seamier tabloids, was impossible to contemplate.

Having rationalised the situation, accepted it with the logic that was such an intrinsic part of her way of thinking, she was able to meet his eyes squarely, unconsciously lifting her chin and setting her shoulders.

'I accept your stipulation. I can understand that a man in your position needs an heir.'

She thought she had countered him with suitable dignity, admitting no hint of the carnal which his deliberate introduction of the subject of children, and the getting of them, could very well have produced.

But her tongue ran away with her then, panicking, betraying the intimate nature of the thoughts she'd hoped to hide from him.

'But I would like to make one stipulation of my own— that we don't—we don't actually sleep together for, well, a couple of weeks or so after we're married.' She met the cool questioning of his eyes, the slight upward tilt of one strongly defined black brow, and blundered heedlessly on, her gaucheness totally out of character. 'I'd like time to adjust, to get to know you better—as a husband, I mean—before we actually, er——' Words failed her then and he supplied,

'Make love.'

His eyes moved with lazy boldness over her lips, her throat, the sweet, curving line of her shoulders and breasts.

'It's a bargain, Cleo. Two weeks to the day.' And she hung her head, her fingers twisting mindlessly in her lap. It sounded less like a bargain than an awful threat!

They were married quietly three weeks later, and the only people at the sort civil ceremony were Aunt Grace, Luke and Jude's sister Fiona.

It was fitting in a way, Cleo thought as she left the registrar's office on Jude's arm, that there weren't vast throngs of people waiting to celebrate a wedding that had been arranged, on her part through dark necessity, and on his a need, at last, to begin a family to carry on his name, to inherit his vast wealth.

But Grace had been delighted when she'd heard the news, Cleo recalled as she watched her aunt and Fiona climb into Luke's BMW for the drive back to Slade House.

'An excellent match!' That lady had come as near to open enthusiasm as it was possible for her to do. 'It will be good to have the Mescal name so closely allied with the Slades' again.'

And later, Uncle John had told her, 'I'm glad. Glad. You couldn't have made a better choice. I have great faith in young Mescal's judgement—I only wish your father and I had had as much in his uncle's.' He had taken her hand, holding it in an unprecedented display of affection, 'But when your father and I were young we thought we knew it all, so we took the bit between our feet, pulled out of Mescal Slade and founded Slade Securities. We took risks, we had to, and it paid off. Though Grace always thought secondary banking to be socially inferior, I'm afraid. But we made up for that in superior living in every degree—Grace saw to that.' He had sighed then, as if he regretted the breakaway still. 'Yes, it's good to know the two families will be allied again, that "Slade" won't just be a redundant name on a letter heading.'

So everyone was pleased, Cleo thought; even Jude had behaved like a devoted bridegroom-to-be when they'd accepted a dinner invitation at Slade House. Not that she'd seen much of him during the past three weeks. She'd spent most of her time booking him on flights to Zurich, Bonn, New York, arranging his hotel accommodation, fixing meetings with foreign bankers and clients.

'I rather think we should have gone first.' Jude placed a hand on the small of her back, only lightly, but it made her shudder. Today just did not feel like her wedding day. She stared unseeingly at the grey façades of the buildings on the opposite side of the street as if she didn't know where she was, what she was doing. She couldn't bring herself to look at him and Jude enquired softly, feeling that betraying shudder, 'Cold, darling?'

'Yes. Yes, I am, a little.' Cleo grasped at the excuse gratefully. It wouldn't do his ego much good to know that his bride of ten minutes had shuddered like a startled mare because he had touched her! And the weather had changed, feeling more like November than May, and there was little warmth in the cream silk suit she was wearing, little warmth in her heart, but he wasn't to know that.

'Shall we go, then?' The arm he put round her shoulder as he hurried her over the pavement to where the Rolls, minus Thornwood today, was parked was protective, but Cleo felt her whole body go stiff, rejecting even that small intimacy.

But the tug of the wind on her small hat, cream straw decked with apricot roses, came to her rescue, gave her yet another useful excuse in the automatic way both hands fled up, securing the nonsensical headgear, because that instinctive movement effectively knocked his arm away.

He looked down at her as she struggled to secure her hat, tipping it further down over her eyes in the process, and his eyes were light with laughter.

'That scrap of silliness suits you. Makes you look ultra-feminine and in need of protection. It's a side of you that's never on display in the office. I like it!' There was warm appreciation in the way he smiled and Cleo scrambled into the car as he held the passenger door open for her.

She felt a fraud, and she said over her shoulder, trying not to sound stiff, 'You'd think I'd flipped if I turned up for work wearing this!'

She heard his deep chuckle as he walked round the car, and she gritted her teeth. She was as she was, there was nothing more. The coolly sophisticated woman he knew as his PA was all there was to her. She had no frivolous, ultra-feminine side. Would he be disappointed when he realised that?

He slid in beside her and the engine purred aristocratically to life at the start of the journey to Slade House where Grace had arranged a small celebration lunch party for them. Uncle John hadn't been well enough to attend the ceremony, but she'd see him at the house. She wondered, her face white and set, what his reaction would be if he knew exactly why she had married Jude Mescal. But he would never know; that had been the whole point of the exercise.

'You're very quiet, Cleo.' Calm, azure eyes left the road for a split second, probing hers. 'Second thoughts?'

'No, not at all,' Cleo lied. During the past three weeks she'd been having second through to tenth thoughts, but they'd all led to the same inevitable conclusion. She was doing the only thing she could, given cold circumstance.

She would be in a far worse position had Jude refused to marry her, or if she'd got really cold feet and had called the whole thing off. She would just have to make the best of the situation, and she had far too much respect for Jude to allow him to know that his stipulation about a full marriage had her running scared.

'Good,' he said softly, his strong profile relaxed as he returned his full attention to the road. There was even a smile in his voice, and Cleo marvelled that he should appear so much in control, so easy in his mind. He, for one, could have no doubts about their future.

'I've some news for you,' he told her. 'Interested?'

'Of course. Tell me.' Cleo jerked herself out of the dangerous and all too often recurring mood of introspection, and Jude grinned.

'I've managed to fix us a honeymoon on a Greek island. Only a week, I'm afraid, that's all the time I can spare right now. But we'll have time to relax together.' He braked for traffic lights, his hands light on the wheel, and turned to her, his eyes enigmatic, 'It might help you to adjust.'

'It sounds delightful.' She carefully kept her tone neutral, not letting him know she had recognised the specific words she'd used when making her own stipulation. 'But a long way to go for just one week.'

'I suppose so,' he concurred absently. If he was disappointed by her lack of enthusiasm he wasn't showing it. 'But when a colleague offered me the use of his villa, the thought of all that sun, sea and solitude was too tempting to turn down. I'd been thinking along the lines of asking Fiona if we could borrow her cottage in Sussex, but I think we'd enjoy the island better. Besides,' his eyes slanted a totally unreadable message, 'we could both use a break in the sun. We'll leave in three days' time—

give you some breathing space to settle into your new home.'

He was arranging everything with no recourse to her. Was his private persona to be as dominant as his public one? She didn't know whether she liked that idea. But the tiny frown between her eyes was eased away as rapid calculations informed her that they would be back in London before her fortnight's period of grace was up. And then, as if he knew every nuance of her thoughts, every twist and turn of her brain, he added drily, 'To the world at large it will appear as a brief and romantic honeymoon. You can regard it simply as a lazy week in the sun.'

'You've picked yourself a great guy, and I should know! And I just know you're going to be happy.' Fiona was the first to greet them when they reached Slade House. 'Welcome to the family, poppet!'

Cleo was roundly kissed on both cheeks, and her hat slid further down over her nose. Laughing, she took it off and tossed it on a nearby chair, instinctively liking Jude's sister.

After retirement his parents had settled in New Zealand, so Jude had told her, leaving Fiona as his only effective family. Cleo hadn't missed the pride in his voice as he'd talked of his sister. She was lovely to look at, strong-minded, and at thirty years of age she was still unmarried because she preferred the uncomplicated single state, putting all her energies into her nationwide string of boutiques.

'The Mescals don't take lightly to the state of matrimony,' Jude had commented after giving Fiona's potted biography, and that had left Cleo wondering why the Slade Securities shares had been important enough to make him finally plunge into the married state—something he had carefully avoided before.

The shares would be useful to him, but important? Well, fairly. That important? Very unlikely—unless there was something she had missed. Later, she had come to the conclusion that she must have missed something. Jude's brain was clever, quick, and, astute in City matters as she liked to think she was, she knew that his grasp of financial affairs left her as far behind as a snail trailing in the wake of a comet.

Granted, he had decided that the time had come to start a family, but he could have had his pick of women only too eager to have his ring on their wedding fingers. So those shares had to be far more important than she had imagined.

Looking at him across her aunt's beautifully arranged lunch-table, Cleo's heart performed a series of totally disconcerting acrobatics. Fear, she supposed, sipping Dom Perignon to steady herself, fear of the consequences of the chain of events which had led to this day, this moment of sitting opposite a brand new husband— a man whose mind she had grown to know well, to respect and admire, but whose body was a stranger, a stranger she was going to force herself to learn to know.

Oh, dear heaven! She dabbed at her mouth with her white linen napkin, not allowing for one moment that the flip and flop of her heart might have anything whatsoever to do with the sheer masculine charisma of the man whose lithely muscled body was covered with such easy and understated elegance by the fine, dark grey fabric of a formal suit, impeccably white shirt and pearl-grey tie.

Dragging her eyes away from him, she slid a sideways smile to Simmons who, impassive as ever, replaced the plate a housemaid had moved with an oval platter bearing a thick, succulent steak of sea-trout. And while the performance was repeated around the table she caught Jude's eyes, swallowed her breath at the cool directness in those azure depths and turned quickly away, fastening her attention on Grace, who was unusually animated, chatting between Luke, Fiona and John. And Cleo wondered if what her uncle had said regarding her aunt's disapproval of the way the break between them and Mescal Slade had come about had any bearing on her coldness towards herself.

People were complicated creatures, present actions and attitudes often stemming from the effects of the past— even if they didn't realise it themselves. It made them incapable of acting differently. Cleo could no more blame her aunt for her cool rigidity towards the daughter of the man who had, in her opinion, enticed her husband away from the more socially acceptable world of merchant banking than she could blame a hedgehog for having prickles.

'I think we ought to attempt a little light conversation, don't you?' Jude's cool, soft voice splintered her solitary thoughts as he laid a hand over hers, imprisoning her fingers as she absently played with the stem of her wineglass. The sensation of skin on skin, of the tensile strength of those long, square-ended fingers, made her catch her breath. Her teeth sank into her lower lip and Jude said, 'Don't scream, you're safe for another two weeks, my dear,' then commanded, a trace of acid in his voice, 'Smile for me. Or is that too much to ask?'

And because she sensed the others were watching, their conversation broken while they turned their attention to the newly weds, who surely should be looking ecstatic, Cleo pinned a brilliant smile on her face, then felt like crying because she could see by the sudden bleakness in his eyes that he knew just how false it was.

* * *

'There's a gentleman to see you, madam.' Meg stood in the doorway of the study where Cleo had just finished a phone call to an estate agent about the marketing of her home in Bow. She frowned, wishing Meg wouldn't insist on that formal, ageing mode of address. 'Call me Cleo, or Mrs Mescal, if you can't manage that,' she had instructed when she had arrived here as Jude's bride two days ago. But Meg, friendly and co-operative as she was, wasn't having that. Meg was of the old school, and that was that!

'Oh—put him in the drawing-room.' Cleo closed her notepad and pushed her fingers through her hair, asking belatedly, 'Who is it?'

'A Mr Robert Fenton, madam. He said it was urgent.' Meg sniffed, her expression showing that in her opinion nothing could be urgent enough to keep the new mistress of the house from what she should be doing—getting ready for her honeymoon! 'Shall I tell him you're too busy? Ask him to leave a message? There's all the packing still to be done for tomorrow.'

'No, I'll see him.' Cleo turned, able now to smile briefly at the housekeeper. At the mention of that hated name she had gone icy cold, averting her head and pretending to search through a drawer in the desk for something. Now, her scrabbling fingers were stilled, her features composed, or reasonably so, she hoped. She had to see the creature some time, she knew that, but had hoped that their next contact would be by letter or telephone.

But she could be thankful for small mercies because at least Jude was out, enmeshed in paperwork back at the office, she told herself as she walked through the hall as steadily as she could on disgracefully trembly legs. She could thank heaven, too, that Jude had insisted she use the day or two before they left for that Greek island to get better acquainted with her new home and begin the disposal of her old one. Had he not, then that snake Fenton might have tracked her down to the office, and that would have taken some explaining away.

Suddenly, though, and with a depth that shook her, she longed for the reassuring presence of the man she had married; longed for his strength, for the gentleness that had been the hallmark of the sensitive way he had handled their ambiguous relationship ever since they had arrived here after the wedding lunch at Slade House.

Jude, I need you! The words took wing in her mind, echoing, and she bit her lips in exasperation for the maudlin, weakly character those silent words conjured up.

She needed him here, at this precise moment, like she needed a sledgehammer to drop on her head from a great height! What he would have to say if he discovered she was being blackmailed, and why, would make a Colossus quake! And she wasn't weak, not weak at all!

Squaring her shoulders, she opened the drawing-room door and walked quickly through and Robert Fenton drawled, 'May I offer my congratulations on your marriage, Mrs Mescal?'

Cleo ignored that, although she felt her face, her whole body, go hot. The mere sight of him made her blood boil.

'Don't come here again, under any circumstances,' she told him, her eyes letting him know how much he disgusted her. To think she had once found him charming company! To think—— But no, her brain shifted gear, moving swiftly, decisively; she must not think of the past. It was done with, over. Or almost. This creep meant less than nothing to her now. She loathed and despised him, and the act of handing over a sum of money would rid herself of the poison that was Robert Fenton finally and for ever.

'I won't—if I don't have to.' His eyes were nasty, his mouth curved in a sneer. He had helped himself to a large measure of Jude's brandy, she noted savagely. And to see him here, lounging on Jude's sofa and drinking his brandy, turned her stomach. But she had her rage under control, because to rant and rail at him might give her temporary relief but it would accomplish nothing useful.

So she said tonelessly, 'There was no need for you to come here today. A telephone call would have done.'

'Would it, now?' He mocked her careful dignity. Swirling the contents of his glass, he leaned back, his smile deadly. 'I'd like to see you try to feed twenty-five thousand smackers down a telephone line.'

'I haven't got it yet.' Cleo's hands balled into tight fists. But she trod warily, guessing how nasty he would become if he weren't reassured that the money he demanded would be forthcoming. 'I have been married for two days. Things can't move that quickly. As soon as I can, I'll let you have it. I don't want this sordid business hanging over my head any longer than necessary.'

'How soon? Next week?' he asked, his eyes sharp, and Cleo dragged in a deep breath, feeling the wetness of sweat on her forehead, the palms of her hands, her back.

'No. The week after. We're leaving tomorrow on our honeymoon.' Sharing any details of her life with him made her feel ill and the words were stiff, difficult to push past her teeth. 'Leave me a phone number. I'll contact you when I have it.'

'Just see you do.' He had pushed himself to his feet, moving to stand close, and Cleo was too frozen with loathing to move away, her feet rooted to the silky oriental carpet. 'Because, quite apart from poor old Uncle John, you have someone else to consider now, don't you, my love?' An eyebrow arched with hateful mockery. 'The sort of stuff I could dish out about you would make that new husband of yours look something of a laughing-stock in the City, wouldn't it? A bit of a fool, wouldn't you say? And he wouldn't be one bit pleased, would he?'

She couldn't speak; there was nothing to say. But she longed to lash out at him, to hit, kick and batter, but the moment of temper, of hot temptation, passed. And Fenton drawled, 'Yes, we must consider your husband's feelings in all this, mustn't we, my love—my clever, clever love? And you are clever, damably so. I admire you for it! To get your pretty little hands on a large fortune, you marry an even larger one! Nice thinking! Go right to the top of the class!'

And behind them, in a voice that would have frozen a molten lava flow, Jude said, 'Won't you introduce me to your friend, darling?'

And Cleo, her eyes darkening with panic, watched with horrified fascination as Robert Fenton gave her a leering wink over the rim of the brandy glass he was lifting to his lips.

CHAPTER FOUR

AFTERWARDS, Cleo had been unable to remember precisely how she'd coped. Her heart had been slamming, her stomach clenched in a sickening knot, but she'd managed to perform the introductions gracefully although she'd been agonisingly aware of Jude's eyes on her as she'd watched, as though mesmerised, as his brandy had slid down Fenton's throat.

'Can't stay, I'm afraid,' Fenton had handed the empty glass to Cleo, his eyes flickering to Jude as he swaggered to the door. 'Just dropped in to offer my congratulations. Lovely lady you have, Mescal. Quite lovely.'

'I'll see you out.'

Jude's voice had been toneless as he'd followed the other man out through the door, ignoring Fenton's airy, 'No need, I can find my way.'

And Cleo had sagged against the wall, still clutching the empty glass, her hands shaking. How much had Jude heard? Panicking, she tried to force her mind to remember exactly what Fenton had been saying. Something about how clever she'd been to marry Jude's fortune in order to get her hands on her own! He would think she'd been bragging about it—and to Fenton, of all people—and plying him with the best brandy to add insult to injury!

Quickly, she put the glass on a table, drawing in deep breaths and trying to compose herself as she heard Jude's approaching steps along the hall.

'Known him long?'

The enquiry was almost polite and she said, 'About two years,' searching his eyes for a clue to his mood. But there was nothing, just a blank careful coolness, only a hint of a question in the gravelly voice.

'Just called to offer his congratulations?'

'Yes, that's right.' She was sure he must hear the lie in her voice, see it in her eyes, and she had turned away, rearranging an already perfectly balanced bowl of tulips, feeling the cool, waxy petals beneath her shaking fingers, waiting for the accusation that must come if he had indeed overheard the remark Fenton had made.

But there had been nothing, and, when she'd steeled herself to look around, the room had been empty.

And now the sun beat down from a paintbox-blue sky, shimmering on the fine golden sand, bouncing off the cluster of angular white buildings of the fishing village further down the coast.

Cleo stirred, stretching her long legs, revelling in the heat of the sun, and Jude said, so very casually, 'Turn over. You've had as much sun on your back as your skin can stand.'

Her heart picking up speed, Cleo's body went rigid and wary, very still. She hadn't heard him come over the sand. But then she wouldn't, would she? The sand was very soft and she'd been drowsing, and the hypnotic suck and drag of the waves as they lapped the shore and retreated again would have drowned out any sound he might have made.

Then he spoke again, repeating his directive, his voice sharper this time.

Recognising the sense of his command, Cleo turned, feeling the beach towel rumple beneath her, wishing she'd been more prepared. She still trod carefully through the minefield of uncertainties, unspoken anxieties, that was her week-old marriage to this man.

She fumbled for her sunglasses and put them on, something to hide behind. There was little else. Her tiny black bikini revealed most of what there was to reveal, and she wouldn't have worn it if she'd known he would be back from that fishing trip so soon. She had imagined she had the best part of the day to herself.

'You're back early.' So light her voice, so carefully neutral. Cleo was proud of the way she was containing those creeping, unnerving anxieties, the doubts, the dread. He was looming over her and she snapped her eyes away. Dressed in only a pair of brief black denim shorts—faded and ragged—the dark golden body which was dusted with crisp black hair seemed impossibly male, superbly athletic and very, very threatening. The sight of him made something inside her shudder, tremble with a sensation she couldn't identify. It was fear, she told herself, primitive fear. But there was something more, something nameless.

'I didn't want to be accused of neglecting my wife.' There was a bite to his tone that she hadn't heard during the week of their marriage, and she sensed a difference in his attitude. A subtle difference that made her feel tense, more wary than ever.

It had been as much as she could do to adequately cope with the way he had been since their wedding: cool, polite, but pleasant with it. And the four days they'd been on the island hadn't been quite the ordeal she'd anticipated. He had been courteous, making sure she was content, had all she needed. And what the maid, who apparently came with the villa, thought about the arrangement of separate bedrooms, the way they spent most of their days following separate pursuits, Cleo didn't know, or care.

She clung gratefully to that separate room, her own private space, like a child counting and re-counting those last few precious days of a school holiday, because she had seen the way he looked at her from time to time, seen it and instinctively known what that look meant. He was a normal, virile male, after all, and she was his wife.

But if he was going to be tetchy because there was another week to go before he could, with honour, claim his conjugal rights—the very phrase made her squirm— then she didn't know how she could bear it. And she didn't know how she would bear it when she would be expected to share his bed. Close her eyes and think of England, she supposed! And——

'Eeek!' she yelped, her dreary thoughts sharply interrupted by a sensation of cold squelchiness, then of warmth and strength as Jude's hand began to massage sun-cream into the soft, heated skin of her naked midriff.

'I can do that!' she gabbled, galvanised into action and struggling to sit up. A mistake, she realised; his hand was now trapped between her updrawn thighs and her breasts.

Smoky grey eyes, wide behind dark lenses, winged sideways apprehensively, met his, and held. His ebony-fringed eyes were as blue as the improbably blue sea that sucked at the shore and, like the sea, contained small depths of clear emerald, brilliant flecks of light. The glinting lights of laughter, damn it!

He was laughing at her, not openly, but inside—which made it worse. Laughing at her foolishly coy and virginal behaviour, making her feel foolish, clumsy and gauche.

'I know you can do it.' His husky voice came close to her ear, his breath fanning her skin as he leaned forward, prising his hand from its softly sensual trap and laying her prone on the towel again. 'But so can I, so why not just stop twittering, and lie back and enjoy?' he added, his words pricking her mind on different levels.

Other than lashing at him with hands and feet, there was nothing she could do. And fighting him physically would achieve exactly nothing. He could, if he wished, flatten her with one hand, the muscled strength of his naked torso left her in no doubt about that at all! Besides, it would be undignified, and it would make him think he had a hell-cat for a wife. He didn't deserve that.

And so she gritted her teeth and endured, and closed her eyes and tartly reminded herself that she had to get used to such liberties, liberties that in exactly one week's time would sharply escalate up the scale of intimacy!

They had made a bargain and she had too much respect for him, and for herself, not to keep her side of it, and she wondered whether to try self-hypnosis. Not very hopeful as to the outcome, especially when the self-prescribed treatment was instigated in a moment of panic, but willing to try anything, she silently repeated, 'I will be a good wife. I will. I will.' And eventually the silent exhortation assumed the soothing rhythm of the sea, of the gentle pressure of his hands as he massaged the cream on to her long, slender legs.

A pulse began to flutter in her throat as his fingers feathered the soft skin of her inner thigh, accelerating as his plundering fingers took more than was honest when they slid a little way beneath the fabric of the tiny triangle which made the bottom half of her bikini. Agonisingly, she felt every muscle and sinew of her body clench in a spasm of purely instinctive rejection, but the thieving fingers moved onwards, towards more legitimate areas, covering the flat plane of her stomach, the soft flare of her hips, the arch of her ribcage.

And to Cleo it suddenly began to feel like nothing she had ever experienced before. Frightening—but obviously not frightening enough! Her mind told her to defend herself against the marauder, but her body had definite ideas of its own, was acquiescent, limpid. And she was drowning in something warm and deep, and not really painlessly because her lungs felt tight, as if she should be gasping for air, and her heart was pattering wildly... And any self-defensive thoughts she might have had were being subdued by his lean, knowing hands, and she knew that if she allowed herself to relax, by just that necessary fraction, she would be completely and utterly subjugated...

When his fingers found the front fastening of her bra top, moving aside the two small halves to expose the twin rounded peaks to the sun, to his eyes, to his hands, she made an effort to protest, to tell him, acidly, that she was unlikely to get sunburned just there, especially if he could refrain from interfering with her clothing! But the words just wouldn't come out coherently. They emerged thickly, like a moan, a moan of pleasure. And as she felt her nipples harden as a tug of something sweet yet achingly fierce flared to life deep inside her, she knew that the fraction of relaxation had been achieved, that the erotic, wordless lovemaking of his hands had dissolved the very last barrier... He was her man, her mate, and she wanted him as she had never wanted anything before. And without conscious design her body arched sensually beneath his hands, a blatant invitation, and he said, 'That should do it.'

The clipped, disinterested tones came as if from a very great distance and it was several seconds before Cleo realised that the sweet ache inside her, the sensual and unstoppable need he had aroused, was to remain an ache. A sour ache.

He was standing up now, his lithe body taut, a glistening bronze masterpiece in the bright Greek sunlight, totally imperious and quite unmoved by what had happened to her because, quite obviously, nothing had happened to him.

He began to unzip his shorts and Cleo closed her eyes, her throat tightening as he told her blandly, 'I'm going for a swim. See you.' And when she opened her eyes again he had gone.

She searched the water and found him, cleaving through the deep blue depths in a powerful crawl, and she scrambled to her feet, her fingers shaking as she re-fastened her bra top then gathered her things together, pushing them in her beach bag.

Her face was burning, and it wasn't from the effects of the sun. It was shame. Shame and humiliation both. He, no doubt bored by this empty charade of a marriage, but bound by his agreement to her stipulation, and irritated to the point of exasperation by the way she had previously skittered nervously away from the slightest physical contact, had taken the opportunity to demonstrate just how he could, if he wished, subdue her.

And he had done so, and to add the final telling insult had walked away, showing her how completely unmoved he was by her obvious arousal. He could take her or leave her—that was the message his actions had transmitted, loud and clear.

She didn't think she would ever forgive him for that. Ever. And the ease with which he had physically dominated her would make her shy away from him in the future more than ever before!

Back at the white one-storey villa Cleo helped herself to a tall glass of fresh lemon juice from the jug in the fridge, gulping it down thirstily, her stormy eyes darting around the cool gleaming kitchen as if she expected someone to leap out of the shadows and attack her.

Someone? Jude, of course! His hands on her body had been a form of attack—insidious, almost unbearably erotic, but an attack all the same!

But gradually she relaxed, her eyes calmer, her hands almost steady as she rinsed her glass. Jude would be back on the beach, or still swimming. Either way, she had again put distance between them. However, a nasty little voice intoned maliciously, deep in her brain, she wouldn't always be able to keep her distance. And he wouldn't always draw back at the moment of capitulation, not if he wanted children, he wouldn't.

And beginning a family had been the reason he had decided to marry, and the Slade Securities shares had meant that she had been the woman he had chosen to bear his children. Suddenly, the idea was mortifying. She had thought she was doing the right and sensible thing when she'd suggested they marry, but now she wasn't so sure. She seemed to be pulling herself out of one mess, only to find herself entangled in one which was worse!

She had always admired Jude for his ability to remain aloof, cool, and for the way he was always in total control. But as she flounced from the kitchen and down a cool corridor to her room she could see the other side of that ability of his—the darker, cruel side.

The way he had shown her how he could bring her to the point of begging for his lovemaking—despite the absence of the love she had always believed to be essential—had left her shaking with unfulfilled need and self-disgust. A potent mixture, poisonous. And that very ability of his, which she had once so admired, now sickened and frightened her.

Stripping off her bikini, she hurled it into a corner of the spacious, traditionally furnished bedroom she was using and padded to the en suite bathroom to stand under the shower, sluicing away every last trace of the sun-cream, as if his fingerprints still lingered in the oily substance. She hoped that their children, when they arrived, would look like her—grey-eyed blondes—with not one trace of their father's dark, cruel beauty. They would be her children, not his! Hers! She would make them so, and that would be the final irony. She hated him at this moment, she really did, she didn't want to give him one damned thing—not even children that resembled him in the slightest!

Cleo heard the maid arrive in time to prepare the evening meal, bringing the fresh fish, fruit and vegetables she bought in the village each day.

Edgy, she put aside the book she'd been trying to read and walked from the terrace through the arched doorway that led to her room, pushing the silvery tumble of silky hair back from her face.

Jude was late. It only ever took the middle-aged Greek woman an hour to make their meal, sometimes less. So where was Jude?

Catching sight of the frown-line between her huge grey-eyes, she turned away from the revealing mirror reflection. She couldn't actually be worried about him, could she? A few hours earlier she hadn't cared if she never saw him again!

But she was calmer now and knew she had overreacted. He had made her want him. So? He was her husband, wasn't he? That she was fastidious and had always believed she would have to love a man before she could be sexually aroused was something she had taken for granted. But he had aroused her, revealing a depth of sexuality she hadn't known she possessed. She was learning things about her character that alarmed her, but that didn't mean she had to go over the top.

And she was learning things about Jude, too. That he was male enough, arrogant enough, to need to lay claim to his ownership, to let her know that he could make her want him whenever he felt like doing so.

Restless now—where was the man?—she riffled through the few garments she'd brought with her and eventually selected a silky amethyst calf-length dress and laid it on the bed, then paced back to the terrace to stare out along the deserted beach.

Since they had been here they had always met on the terrace at this time in the evening. Usually they had spent the daytime hours at separate ends of the island, because he seemed no more anxious for her undiluted company than she was for his. But they always began their evenings here, having a drink or two before dinner, making light, impersonal conversation. And now his absence was making her nervous.

But that in itself was nothing new. He had been making her nervous ever since he had agreed to marry her! And it had grown progressively worse, aggravated by the way he'd said not a word about Robert Fenton's presence in his home, about what he might have overheard when he'd walked in and found them together. This afternoon's episode on the beach had been the final straw!

She paced the terrace, her feet making rapid patterns of sound on the terracotta tiles, the edges of her lacy robe fluttering in a soundless echo of her own agitation as she thought back to the days—now seeming totally unreal—when she had confidently believed herself to be the only person Jude Mescal couldn't make nervous!

And then he was there, in the archway leading from her room, his body relaxed, like the mean and magnificent cat she had always thought he resembled.

He was already dressed for dinner, his narrow black trousers and formal white lightweight jacket fitting him to perfection, making him look suave yet deadly.

'Good book?' His eyes drifted to her discarded novel as he walked, soft-footed, to where she had been sitting earlier, placing the two dry martinis he had brought with him on the low marble-topped table, and Cleo shook with anger, shrugging aside his question with a tight shrug of her shoulders.

It was no use his asking her if the book was a good one; she couldn't remember a word of the few she had read. Mostly she hadn't been reading at all, just sitting here, wondering why he was late, when he would come home. And all the time he had been here, showering, changing, fixing drinks, not bothering to let her know he was in the house. Dammit, she'd actually been worried about the insouciant swine because the last time she'd seen him he'd been swimming out to sea as if the hounds of hell were following him! The man was intolerable!

And she didn't know why he had this power to make her angry because, as his PA, she had always been able to handle him. And he had gained the terrace by coming through her room. He hadn't set foot inside it before now, and that, coming after what had happened this afternoon, made the palms of her hands go slippery with sweat.

Mentally shaking herself for her own foolishness, for the inner agitation she would have to learn to come to terms with, she took the drink he had fixed for her, carrying it over to the stone balustrading of the terrace and staring blindly out to sea.

If she joined him at the table she would have to look at him. She didn't want to meet those clever eyes because she knew she would be able to see in them the mind pictures of the way she must have looked this afternoon when she'd abandoned her practically naked body to the exploration of his hands.

'Cleo——' Her name on his lips sounded, suddenly, quite unbearably intimate, and she reluctantly made a half-turn towards him, hoping he wouldn't notice the way the hand that held her drink was shaking. 'Come and sit down, I want to talk to you.'

'What about?' A rapid but ostentatious glance at her wristwatch. 'It's time I went to change.' So cool her voice, the small half-smile she angled at nothing in particular. She should be winning Oscars! The last thing she needed right now was to have to sit with him and listen to whatever it was he had to say. The memory of the way she'd felt when his hands had stroked and teased her willing body was still much too close.

'You look fantastic as you are.' A slow drift of long azure eyes over her flushed face, the filmy gown, the length of bare, tanned leg, said it all: sexual interest but overlaid with slight amusement because, after all, he'd seen it all before, and more. He'd touched, and could have taken her had he been so inclined. He hadn't, neither then nor now, it seemed, and for Cleo the sexual embarrassment which the drift of his knowing eyes had engendered became the deeper misery of sheer humiliation as he consulted his own watch. It was as if he had taken stock and mentally dismissed her.

'You've got over half an hour before we need go in to eat.' His mouth tilted with heavy irony. 'Do I have to beg for five minutes of my wife's time?'

'I'm sorry.' Flustered, Cleo sat. Put that way, she could hardly refuse, and she sipped her drink, waiting, and he said,

'I think we should consider buying a house in the country. Somewhere close enough to use at weekends. It would be particularly useful after the children arrive.'

His eyes slid over her, making her skin burn. 'What do you think?'

That it was a pity he had to keep harping on about children! That was what she thought! But she could hardly tell him as much. Holding her glass by the stem, twisting it, she stared into the swirling contents unable to meet those knowing, faintly amused eyes.

'There's time for that,' she answered stiffly, 'After all—— ' she made a concession to his mention of all those children she would be expected to bear '—I expect to continue with my job for some time to come. I enjoy it.'

She couldn't imagine him as a family man, making swings in apple trees, playing football or snakes and ladders in front of a log fire while she busied herself darning endless tiny socks in between baking and preserving in some farmhouse-type kitchen. And how many children did he expect her to have, for goodness' sake? And would she be expected to start producing them right away? One litter after another, like a rabbit? Her throat tightened with what she recognised as incipient hysteria, and if she hadn't been so busy trying to control that disgraceful and, up until becoming entangled with him, alien state, she might have taken his ambiguous reply as fair warning.

'The expected sometimes doesn't happen, Cleo——'

She finished her drink in a gulp, her eyes flicking to his and away again because the message contained there was unreadable—or perhaps she wasn't ready to read it. She didn't know. She got to her feet, trying for poise, 'I really must go and change,' she tossed over her shoulder, her smile brittle. 'By all means we can cast our eyes over a few properties, get to know the market for when we seriously want to buy—some time in the future.'

* * *

If he had decided to charm her he was certainly succeeding, Cleo thought, rising from the table where they had lingered in lamplit intimacy over the delicious meal the Greek maid had prepared.

The trouble was, he could so easily disarm her, she realised as he followed her out on to the moonlit terrace, bringing the brandy decanter and two glasses with him.

And to allow herself to be disarmed would be fatal. She didn't want her emotions involved, it would only lead to pain, because he would never become emotionally involved with her, with anyone, as far as she could tell. And she was no masochist. She would keep to the letter of their bargain, but that was as far as it would go.

But as she went to the balustrade to look out over the silvery night, he followed her, placing a hand on her shoulder where the halter neckline of her dress left it bare. And this time she didn't shy away from his touch, even though that touch felt like needles of excitement pricking her skin.

'Cold?' he said. 'Shall I fetch you a wrap?'

She turned, simply to deny any feeling of coldness because for some reason she had never felt warmer in her life. He was close, so close, and even in the shadowy light of the moon she could see he was not quite as implacably cool as he pretended to be.

'No—I'm fine, thanks.' She moved back to the upholstered bamboo loungers, angled around the table, and sat cradling the drink he'd poured for her.

Something was coming to life between them, a vital new growth, but not something known. Not really known, although she could make a fairly accurate guess. But she had to remember, always remember, that this was a marriage of convenience. And then a thought passed through her mind, leaving an annoying footprint, that maybe her motives had been suspect all along the line.

Solving her problem had depended on finding a husband her uncle and aunt, as her guardians, could approve of. But would she have asked Jude to marry her if he'd been fat and bald with a face like a pug and a mind like a geriatric slug? It was a question she wouldn't like to be forced to answer.

The sea was blessedly cool, lapping against her feet as she walked slowly along the water-line, the soft black night hiding her. Not that there would be anyone about at this time of night to see her. The thought comforted her a little, and a small smile tugged at the corners of her mouth as the breeze moulded the almost transparent lawn of her nightdress to the shape of her body.

She hadn't been able to sleep; the night was too hot, her thoughts jumping this way and that, making her mind ache.

That tension between them, that awareness, had been growing throughout the long evening, muddling her. And her 'goodnight' to him had been abrupt, far more terse than usual as she'd left the terrace, making for the solitude of her room.

But if she'd been looking for safe haven she hadn't found it there, and at last she'd slipped down to the beach, noticing the light coming from his room and wondering if he, too, found it impossible to sleep, if he found this marriage, entered into so coolly and objectively, had strange and rather terrifying facets that were only now beginning to reveal themselves.

She had never been drawn to the idea of marriage, the total commitment of love. Love was something she'd learned to do without since she'd lost her parents. Her mind, she supposed, was closed to the concept of it. She had imagined, for a brief span, that she was in love with Robert Fenton—and that had turned out to be an all-time disaster. And she'd emerged from the short period of infatuation recognising that what she'd felt had been a natural reaction to the years of dedicated study, the absence of close family love, the absence of fun and frivolity in her life. It had been a necessary, if unpleasant, part of growing up.

But if she had been looking for love, for a man she could respect, share the rest of her life with, then Jude could have been everything she could want in a man. He had a brilliant mind, was even-tempered—well, mostly—and he was strong, yet capable of tenderness, of deep humanity. He also respected her as an equal, and that counted for much—for more than the sum of his undoubted sex appeal, his wealth and position.

Yes, had she been looking for such a man, for love... A small wave, but higher than the rest, took her unawares, wetting her to her knees, and she stumbled, almost fell, then righted herself and turned and saw him a mere two yards away. Everything inside her seemed to stop, just for a moment, before racing on, the blood thudding through her veins, her heart pattering a demented tattoo.

'Jude——' Her voice was thick, his name dragged from her on a sighing breath that faltered hopelessly, because she had known in that instant when time had stood still for her, when her breath, her very heartbeat, had hung suspended, that she loved this man, had probably been falling in love with him since she'd first set eyes on him. It was almost laughably simple! It had certainly been inevitable.

Moonlight, slow and silver, touched his face, stroked his magnificent body with tender moulding fingers, stopping the breath in her throat.

Naked, save for brief dark swimming shorts, he looked pagan—the dominant male to her feminine fragility—and he said her name, like a question, his shadowed eyes, bereft now of their startlingly vivid colour in this ghostly light, raking her, lingering hungrily on the shape of her, on the aching softness of feminine curves only lightly and tantalisingly concealed beneath gossamer fabric.

'I couldn't sleep.' He moved closer, close enough to touch, and her skin turned to flame with the nearness of his almost naked body as he cupped her face in his hands, his eyes searching hers, revealing the depth of his own wanting.

His body shook with it. She could feel the fine tremors that ran over the taut, glistening skin so near to her own, feel the control as he released her, his fingers feathering lightly down the length of her throat before they fell away, clenched into fists now, revealingly, though she knew she was not supposed to know the effort it had cost him to restrain himself from touching her more intimately.

'I'll walk you back.' His voice was kind, but there was a roughness in it, just below the surface, that told her he wanted her, as she wanted him. 'Perhaps a hot drink might help? Me, too—probably more than the swim I'd decided to take before I saw you along the shore.'

He could have been a father, soothing a wakeful child for all the emotion he allowed himself to show. But Cleo knew better, and she wasn't afraid, not now, because she had at last admitted to herself the fact that she must have unconsciously known for months. She loved him, and that was why her proposal to him had seemed so logical, so right! She had been blind for so long, so convinced that she didn't need or want emotional ties that she hadn't recognised what was happening to her!

But she knew it now, knew that the restrictions she had placed on these early days of marriage must be almost intolerable to a man such as he. And they were intolerable to her, now, quite intolerable.

But, such was his sense of honour, he would make no move towards her until the period of restriction he had agreed to was over. Any move had to come from her.

'Jude——' He was waiting for her, just a step or so ahead now, but he pivoted round as her voice touched him, tense, his skin glistening in the silver light as though drenched with sweat, although the breath from the sea was cooling.

'Make love to me.' The husky ease with which she spoke the words didn't surprise her. They were right, so right, and should have been said so very much sooner. She caught the sound of his sharply indrawn breath and her soul shook with the wonder of this moment, with the simple knowledge of her love for him, with what she read in his eyes as he took the hands she held out to him, folding them inwards against the wall of his chest.

'Are you sure?' His voice was throaty, urgency contained. 'Quite sure?'

And she nodded, too full of love for him to speak, too near to tears, or laughter, because she'd been such a blind fool these last months. She lifted her face to him, and he caught his breath, drawing her closer so that their bodies touched, just; magic was born as after one long and incredibly tense moment their bodies joined, and the softness of her melted into the demanding hardness of him, hands and lips seeking, finding, consuming.

And there on the shore, with the pulse of the sea melding into the rhythm of the blood in their veins, he made love to her with subtlety, with a tender poignancy that made her want to cry.

She loved him so.

CHAPTER FIVE

'You were leaving without saying goodbye!' Cleo's voice was a husky accusation as she stood in the breakfast-room doorway, fastening the belt of her fine voile robe around her narrow waist. And Jude looked up from the breakfast-table, his smile lazy, his azure eyes incredibly sexy.

'Not so. I would have come to wake you before I left.' He put his morning paper aside. 'Shall I ring for Meg to bring your breakfast through?'

'No, thanks.' Cleo pushed a hand through her rumpled silvery hair and sat opposite, helping herself to a morsel of crisp bacon from his plate, eating it from her fingers. She didn't want anyone to intrude, not even Meg, who was one of the most unobtrusive people she knew; she wanted Jude to herself. Never again could she affect to be cool and blasé towards this husband of hers. She loved him so much.

Her only regret was that she couldn't tell him so. He had married her because it was convenient to do so, no other reason. That she had proved to be as sexually eager as he, would, to his logical masculine mind have proved a bonus. To admit her love would embarrass him. He wouldn't want the responsibility of it.

He was looking good, very good, his dark hair, still damp from the shower he must have taken earlier, clinging to his skull, his deep tan contrasting dramatically with the stark whiteness of his shirt. Her fingers ached to touch him. Every morning when she had wakened from luxurious sleep she had reached out for him and he had woken, turning to her, nuzzling her hair and then lazily, languorously, they had made love.

Not this morning, though. It was their first back in London because he'd said, 'What the hell!' contacted Mescal Slade and informed Dawn Goodall that they were taking another week, staying on the island. And this morning she had reached for him and he hadn't been there. Just an empty space between cool sheets, and she'd panicked, remembering he'd said he'd be going to the City today.

Stumbling out of bed, she'd grabbed at her robe, struggling into it as she'd run down the stairs, not wanting him to leave before she'd had a chance to see him, simply see him.

Now, relaxed again because she was with him, she reached for his coffee-cup, cradling it in both hands, sipping while he finished his bacon and eggs, and he asked, 'What are you going to do with yourself today?'

Cleo hunched one shoulder, her mouth curving in a warm, slow smile. 'Go shopping?' she hazarded. For some reason Jude had suggested she take a further week off. She would have preferred to be behind her desk again, close to him, working with him. But he had insisted and she wasn't up to arguing with him about it, about anything, not in this mood of euphoria she wasn't. A dark eyebrow lifted and she elaborated, 'I might get a new dress.' She felt in the mood for celebrating, and buying something exciting would serve. That her ever-deepening love for him was just cause for celebrating she couldn't explain, not yet, so she tacked on, 'We're entertaining the Blairs on Thursday, so I need to pull out all the stops!'

She expected him to comment on the planned dinner party. Sir Geoffrey Blair was chairman of Blair and Dowd Developments, a company that was climbing fast and far, and Jude had been angling for their account. Thursday night could well clinch it. But he growled, leaning over the table to take his coffee-cup from her hands, 'Do you intend to consume all my breakfast, woman?' However, the quirk of his mouth belied the black bar of his lowered brows, and he drank the remains, then refilled the cup, took a mouthful then put the steaming cup back between her hands. 'Henpecked already,' he grinned and she nodded sagely, as if she quite agreed, although she knew that henpecked was the last thing this man would ever be. But their developing relationship admitted this type of gentle teasing and she welcomed it, as she welcomed everything about him.

'Do you know how irresistible you look in that thing?' Lazy eyes swept her, the soft movement of his mouth adding erotic emphasis to the drift of his eyes as they roamed from the spun silver disorder of her hair, her flushed cheeks, the slope of her shoulders, to the swelling roundness of her breasts.

The robe she had pulled on was meant to be worn over a matching nightdress. Worn over nothing at all, its pink transparency was little more than a blush, and Cleo's pulses quickened as the sensual curve of his mouth became more pronounced, his voice a growly inspiration as he whispered, 'Irresistible enough to take you back to bed and let Mescal Slade look after itself.'

For a silent, timeless moment their eyes held, the intimacy almost shocking, and she thought he might just do that, but then she saw the change, the assumption of briskness that told her he had moved away from her, on to a separate plane entirely, and she knew—as if she could ever have doubted it—that work would always take first place for him.

She reluctantly respected him for that, she decided, watching as he shot a glance at his watch. The most she could hope for was that in time she would become as necessary to him as he was to her.

And there was a chance of that, she knew there was. The knowledge was like a small, bright flame inside her, warming her, allowing her to see more clearly ahead. He liked and respected her and he took pleasure in her body, and that was as good a basis as any to build on. And she would build on it, brick by patient brick, be as much to him as he would allow, hide the depth of her own emotional involvement, her total commitment, until he was ready to accept it.

He stood up, reaching for the light grey suit jacket which had been hanging over the back of his chair, shrugging into it, his movements, as ever, sheer male elegance. And Cleo got to her feet, too, longing to go to him, to slip her arms beneath the beautifully tailored jacket and feel the warmth of muscle, sinew and bone through the crisp whiteness of his shirt.

But she wouldn't do that, of course. She couldn't give herself that luxury. Their marriage was a compartmented thing and his mind was now geared to the working day ahead; he wouldn't welcome an untimely display of her physical need of him. It might annoy him, and it would certainly reveal the depth of her emotional involvement.

He picked up his briefcase and she lifted her face to receive his goodbye kiss, an unsatisfying brush of his lips over hers, and she expected that to be that, but he stood for a moment, smiling down at her, making her heart tumble about beneath her ribs.

The character lines on either side of his mouth indented wryly as he held her eyes, and it was all Cleo could do to prevent herself from reaching up and fastening her lips over the superbly crafted lines of his mouth. But she knew she had to be circumspect if this unusual but already beautiful marriage of theirs was to work out, to live and grow. Their relationship was too new, too delicately balanced as yet, to give him one inkling of the way she really felt. He could, at this stage, be horrified by the implications.

Then he touched the side of her face with a slow-moving finger and his eyes were soft.

'I'll give you lunch at Glades. One o'clock.'

Cleo had finished dressing and was half-way down the stairs when Meg came out of the kitchen.

'There's a phone call for you, madam. Luke Slade.'

'Thanks, Meg, I'll take it in the study.'

Cleo responded warmly to the housekeeper's smile. Meg's devotion to Jude had lapped over on her, and the older woman asked, 'Shall I bring your breakfast through, madam? How about a nice boiled egg—free-range and fresh?' she tempted.

Cleo shook her head, admitting, 'I finished off the toast Jude couldn't eat, thanks,' and was aware of Meg's cluck of disapproval as she went to take that call, wondering why Luke had bothered to contact her. He certainly wouldn't be enquiring about her health—they had never got on very well together.

'Cleo?' His voice sounded harsh and tinny. 'Thank God you're back. I was afraid you and Jude might have skived off for yet another week. How soon can you get here?'

His urgency worried her and she asked quickly, 'What's wrong? Not Uncle John?'

But Luke snapped, 'He's fine. Just get here. Fenton's been round, making unpleasant demands. We can't discuss it on the phone. Just get here.'

She arrived at the Slade Securities head office in Eastcheap still in a state of shock, but as she dismissed

Thornwood and the Rolls and walked across the pavement her thoughts began to unlock themselves, tumbling out all over her brain.

In the exquisite delight of recognising her love for Jude, in the joy they had discovered together during those long golden days and jewelled nights, Robert Fenton, and her reason for needing a husband in the first place, had been pushed from her mind, because garbage like that had no place in the ecstatic, the delicate, the passionate act of falling in love.

She had told Fenton they would be away for one week. But Jude had taken two. And Fenton hadn't been able to wait. So his greed had taken him to Luke, to spread his poison, make his threats, turn the screw.

Her hands were wet with sweat as she took the lift to Luke's office. His secretary told her to go right in, her eyes puzzled, sensing something was wrong. Luke was pacing the floor and he shot over to her, slammed the door closed behind her and grated, 'What the hell kind of mess do you think you've got us into? His narrow face was flushed and his hand shook as he took a bottle from the hospitality cupboard and sloshed two inches of Scotch into a glass. 'He walked in here on Thursday with his oily threats and I've been going spare ever since.' He took a long gulp of the neat spirit and told her, 'He said you'd promised to hand over twenty-five thousand pounds last week, for withholding certain information. By Thursday he'd decided you were reneging so he came to me.'

'I'm sorry you had to get mixed up in this.' Cleo slumped weakly on to a chair. 'I forgot. We didn't get back to London until late yesterday afternoon.'

'Sorry?' Luke bared his teeth in a mirthless grimace, his eyes incredulous. 'And how the hell can you forget a thing like that? Or do you have so many blackmailing threats hanging over you that this one just slipped your mind? It wouldn't surprise me,' he jeered, 'you always did seem too good to be true!'

She wanted to walk out there and then, but couldn't afford the luxury, so she asked, tight-lipped, 'Is this as far as it's gone? Just trying to get the money out of you?'

'He'd be lucky!' His mouth twisted. 'And isn't it far enough? Can you imagine what the kind of publicity he's threatening to put around would do to the company—stuff like that can affect confidence. I can't afford to have that happen. In the state we're in, it could finish us.' He sat down heavily. 'If the money isn't in his hands by tomorrow he threatened to go to Father for it, and if that failed he's seeing some newspaper creep— as bent as he is, no doubt. I would have kicked him out of the door, but I knew he had to be telling the truth about what happened between you, otherwise you'd never have agreed to pay up in the first place.'

'He told you everything?' Cleo felt sick and she almost asked for a drink when Luke got up to pour himself another Scotch. But she needed a clear head to contact her bank and ask them to have the money ready for her to collect in the morning, to arrange a meeting place with Fenton.

Luke sat down again, disgust on his face. 'About your affair, the debts he ran up trying to give you a good time, your promise to marry him, the night you spent together at some out of the way hotel just before you gave him the boot.'

And Cleo said tiredly, 'It wasn't like that. We did date, but it never got heavy and I soon woke up to the fact that all he wanted from me was a share in the Slade Millions.'

'So why did you agree to pay up?' Luke sneered. 'If your relationship was that innocent he wouldn't have had a thing to hold over you. You've got to be as guilty as hell. Not that it bothers me,' he added spitefully. 'I couldn't care less if you have to pay him to hold his tongue for the rest of your life. But I don't go a bundle on being personally threatened by a creep like Fenton. Anyway,' his eyes glittered triumphantly, 'if your relationship was so pure, what about the night you spent together at that Red Lion place? He said he could prove you'd shared a room as man and wife.'

'And so he could,' Cleo agreed wearily. 'We went for a drive in the country—he'd asked me to marry him, secretly, and I turned him down because by that time I knew he was primarily interested in the money I'd eventually inherit. He seemed to take my refusal well, said he hoped we could still be friends. God, I was green!' Her brows knitted over cloudy grey eyes. 'I'd already realised he was a bit of a con-man, but I didn't know he could be evil. I don't know why I'm explaining all this to you, but he engineered the whole Red Lion episode. He booked us in as man and wife and when I found out it was too late to do anything about it. But I spent the night in an armchair. Fenton and I have never been lovers——'

'Yet you're willing to pay out that kind of money!'

Cleo saw the sneering disbelief in his eyes and she said grittily, 'I can't prove we weren't lovers. He can prove we shared a hotel room for a night. I can't disprove his lies—that I said I'd marry him, made him spend money on me he couldn't afford then walked away when he got into debt. And I've found——' her eyes lashed him scornfully '—that most people prefer to believe the worst of others.'

He didn't even look uncomfortable, she noted bitterly, and she punched her message home,

'Had I been the only person concerned I would have told him to go to hell before I gave him a penny. I've no doubt at all that he could have got the whole pack of lies into some grotty scandal sheet, and it wouldn't have done my career much good, but I would have survived. But your father wouldn't. He's old and he's sick, and that type of publicity would finish him. He couldn't take it, and why should he, if I can prevent it? He's always been good to me and he showed me more affection—more understanding, I should say—than you or your mother ever did.'

She reached for her black alligator-skin handbag, fitting the fine shoestring strap over her arm. 'I'm paying up because I owe it to your father, because he was the only person who cared a rap for me after my parents died. And for no other reason.'

'And you married Jude to get your hands on the wherewithal? I thought the whole thing was a bit sudden.'

Luke got to his feet as she made for the door and she told him icily, barely turning her smooth, silvery head, 'I married Jude because I love him.' And it was the truth. She had been falling in love with Jude for a long time, but love was an emotion she had learned to live without. When it had happened it had taken her a long time to recognise it. But that was no business of Luke's.

'So you'll get in touch with Fenton?' Luke was just behind her as she reached the door, and he sneered, 'If it weren't for the trouble that kind of publicity could give Slade Securities I'd happily pay Fenton to spread the dirt.'

'You'd what?' Cleo went cold. 'I don't believe I'm hearing this!'

'You heard,' he drawled, his mouth curling. Cleo knew he'd always resented her, but she hadn't realised that over the years the resentment had deepened to hate.

'Why?'

'There was enough pious fuss from my father when he'd had his attention drawn to that relatively harmless piece about me,' he said bitterly. 'It was even said that it caused his latest heart-attack. So I'd like him to know that Wonder Girl isn't as perfect as he thought she was. It might just put your nose out of joint. He's always holding you up as an example.'

Cleo's mouth went dry as she stared at the cousin she had thought she knew, realising that she didn't know him at all. His cloak of pompous indifference had hidden his hatred. She half turned, her disgust and anger burning her up, and grated, 'You'd want that, even though you know what it would do to your father? He damn near died when he read about the brawl you got yourself involved in. You can't think anything of him at all—you selfish bastard!'

The feeling of rage and disgust kept her going, but even that evaporated completely as she stood in a call box after contacting her bank, phoning Robert Fenton. She felt slightly sick and trembly as she slid into her seat at the table Jude had reserved for them at Glades.

'You're looking tired,' he said after he'd handed back the menus and given their order. Concern clouded the vivid blue of his eyes. 'Bad morning shopping? Or did your visit with Luke upset you for some reason?'

It had been a bad morning, and how, but she couldn't tell him why so she shrugged, putting on a smile, 'So-so,' then, wondering, 'How did you know I'd gone to see Luke?'

'I telephoned home. Meg told me Thornwood had driven you to Eastcheap. A simple deduction.' He looked amused and he leant his elbows on the small linen-covered table-top, trailing the fingers of one hand softly down the curve of her cheek. 'Pretty—pretty and soft,' he murmured, and her heart lurched over with love for him. And as the feathering caress moved over her mouth she parted her lips, closing them over his fingertip, nipping gently, then drew back, her face hot. Never in a million years would she have imagined herself and the chief executive of Mescal Slade making such a public display of themselves!

'Why did you try to reach me?' she asked then, creditably cool, trying to get things back on a more manageable level because if she didn't, and he kept eating her with his eyes, then she would certainly end up making an even more public display of her love for him! She needed him, needed his tenderness, after the battering she'd taken this morning.

And Jude removed his elbows from the table, leaning back as their first course arrived.

'No particular reason. I just needed to hear your voice.' And that made her feel good, so very good, and it melted away some of the distaste which had been produced by this morning's conversation with Luke.

Then, without knowing why, because she and Jude never talked about the circumstances of their marriage, she asked lightly, toying with a forkful of chicken in a light wine sauce, 'Why did you agree to marry me, Jude?'

'Because, as you pointed out, I would always be in the happy position of knowing you hadn't married me for my money. Call me a cynic if you like, but I've never been able to distinguish between people who liked me for what I am and those who just like the smell of wealth.'

It was a flippant reply but it told her he was probably as far away from loving her as he had been when she'd proposed. And that was daunting, but she wasn't going to let it worry her too much. And at least he'd had the sensitivity not to mention the shares, because although they had probably been his first consideration when agreeing to marry her, she didn't want to hear him say as much. It would put what they did have together down on the level of a purely commercial agreement.

She didn't know why she had asked that question, and she didn't know what she'd expected him to say. She hadn't really hoped he would tell her he'd suddenly realised, over that weekend he'd taken to think it over, that he was madly in love with her, had she?

Of course she hadn't. She didn't believe in miracles, and she knew that if he were ever to grow to love her then the process would take time. So why was she now feeling so empty inside?

And he smiled at her lazily, as if they'd been discussing nothing more important than the state of the weather, and lifted the bottle the waiter had left in the cooler at the side of the table. 'Let me give you some wine. I think you'll like it.'

And she smiled, just slightly, because suddenly smiling was difficult. 'Thank you.' She knew that, for him, although their marriage of convenience was working out well so far, it would remain just that, a marriage of convenience, for some long time to come.

Lifting her eyes to him over the rim of her glass, she smiled again, put more into it this time, making herself sparkle. After all, she was a fighter, a stayer, and one day she'd damn well *make* him fall in love with her!

Because, if he didn't, her life might well become unbearable.

CHAPTER SIX

'So I suppose you'll be buying up Harrods this afternoon, as you spent the morning with Luke?' Jude queried as he escorted her from the restaurant, his hand under her elbow, making her feel safe and protected.

'Just a dress.' Cleo smiled quickly. She'd forgotten she'd said she'd be going shopping this morning, Luke's phone call had driven it out of her mind, and she still went cold when she remembered the hatred she'd later seen in his eyes, his bitter resentment.

'Give Thornwood a ring when you've finished, he can collect you. That's what he's paid for.' His eyes warmed, holding hers briefly before he hailed a cruising taxi. 'I don't want a worn-out wife in my bed tonight.'

Cleo wasn't in the mood for shopping, and as she turned into Bond Street her thoughts were miserably chewing over the interview with her cousin that morning. Perhaps she'd always subconsciously known that his dislike of her went deeper than mere resentment, and perhaps that was why she hadn't even thought about approaching him for advice when Fenton had made his first blackmailing demands.

She stared unseeingly into shop windows until she realised she had to snap herself out of this mood of introspection. She had always known that her aunt and cousin had little time for her, were unwilling and unable to absorb her into the family. But Uncle John cared about her, and she had Jude, and Jude had become everything to her.

Things were looking good, she assured herself, and there was real hope for their marriage. It would succeed, and one day he would love her as she loved him. On that she was quite determined! And tomorrow, after she'd paid Fenton off, she would be able to put the past behind her and concentrate all her energies on the most important thing in her life—her marriage to Jude.

An hour later she walked out of a boutique, mingling with the crowds on the pavement. The dress she had bought was more daring than her usual choice. It was calf-length, with a full, soft skirt, in ice-blue—which made the most of her recently acquired tan. So far, so good, but the front of the bodice dipped lower than anything she had ever worn before and the back was non-existent—except for the band of the halter strap around the neck. The quiver of inner excitement she experienced as she imagined Jude's reaction when he saw her in the dress brought a dreamy smile to her lips. And someone said, just behind her, 'Been buying something super?'

Cleo turned, smiling down into the eyes of Polly Masters. Polly worked in the Equity and Research department at Mescal Slade and Cleo asked, 'Day off?'

'Umm. A couple of days, actually.' Her brown eyes slid to the classy carrier Cleo was holding. 'I want to buy a summer suit, but I couldn't afford the prices they charge in that place. You look great, by the way, a tan suits you—and the whole building's still buzzing over the way you upped and married the Frozen Asset. Ooops!' Polly clapped a hand over her mouth, looking mortified. 'Me and my big mouth!'

'I think I may have thawed him a little,' Cleo grinned, and felt proud, and deliriously happy because it was the truth. And everything was almost perfect, and one day, in the not-too-distant future, she hoped it would be completely, utterly perfect.

'Well, bully for you! No one knew there was a big romance going on under our noses. Ouch!' she winced as a passer by knocked into her, nearly sending her flying. 'Tell you what, why don't we grab a coffee, have a natter? We've been having a collection for a wedding present for you and Jude—I mean, Mr Mescal—and he said you'd drop in one day next week—he'd arrange which day with you—and we could do the presentation bit then. Have you retired, or something?' Her head tilted to one side, 'I wish I could. I fancy myself as a Kept Woman!'

'No such thing!' Cleo was quick to scotch that rumour. Polly was a small fish in Equity and Research but she had a large mouth, and Cleo was going to be behind her desk first thing on Monday morning, if not sooner, because idling around was nice and relaxing—or would be when the vile business with Fenton was over—but she couldn't wait to start working with Jude again. 'OK, we'll have that coffee.' She didn't want one, not after her delicious lunch with Jude, but it would give her the opportunity to make it clear to Polly that retirement was the last thing on the cards. She was still Jude's PA and she had no intention of giving up that coveted position.

At the cramped table in the tiny restaurant, Polly picked up the menu. 'I haven't had lunch yet and my stomach thinks my throat's been cut—do you mind?'

'No, of course not, go ahead,' said Cleo. 'I'll just have tea.'

'Well, I'm glad you're not aiming to be a lady of leisure,' Polly confided when she'd given her order. 'Word had it you were resigning, and when Sheila Bates from Takeovers and Mergers heard she nearly flipped. She fancies her chances as your successor! Oh, she's qualified,' Polly twisted a springy black curl around her index finger, her head on one side. 'But she's a pain in the neck. As your husband's PA she'd be insufferable.'

'There's no question of my resigning,' Cleo denied firmly. But something cold wriggled around inside her all the same. Jude had been adamant about her staying away from the office for the rest of this week, and that could have been consideration on his part, because she did have a lot to attend to—clearing up at the house in Bow, deciding what to do about the furniture. But why had he said she'd be dropping in one day next week when he'd been approached about the presentation of the wedding gift? He had obviously made it sound as though she wouldn't be around on a permanent day-to-day basis.

'And talking about Takeovers and Mergers——' Polly's brown eyes were avid as she looked up from her tuna salad. 'A client phoned me yesterday morning, and this guy said he'd heard a rumour that we're making a takeover bid for your uncle's company, Slade Securities. He wanted to know if he should buy in.' A morsel of tuna disappeared between her glossy red lips and Cleo's heart did a small somersault. Her uncle's firm—the largely family-owned company—to be swallowed up by Mescal Slade? It would break his heart, make all the years he and her father had spent building the business up from scratch seem like a waste of time. And Polly said, 'I thought you'd like to know what was in the wind. Why don't you get on to someone in Takeovers and Mergers, find out what's going on. Know what I mean? You could come up with something interesting.'

It was no secret that Cleo's father and Jude's uncle, direct descendants of Harry Slade and Reuben Mescal who had founded the merchant bank way back in the eighteen hundreds had quarrelled. It had happened a long time ago, almost fifty years ago to be exact, and Cleo's father had sold out his shares to Jude's uncle and had gone into secondary banking, founding Slade Securities with his younger brother, Cleo's Uncle John.

When her father had died ten years ago Uncle John had carried on the by then successful company until the second of his heart-attacks had forced him into retirement. Now Luke was at the helm, and if Mescal Slade were considering a takeover bid...

And why hadn't Jude told her? Surely she had a right to know? He would have the final say in any such decision; the board was like putty in his hands. They respected his judgement too much, and with good reason, to do more than superficially question his decisions—and then only for the look of it...

'Hey!' Polly snapped her fingers under Cleo's nose. 'Come on back here—you looked miles away!'

Cleo glanced at the other girl with a start, her eyes unfocused, then smiled automatically, picking up her cup to finish her tea and Polly, eyeing the slenderly cut suit in fine olive green crêpe Cleo was wearing over a white silk V-necked blouse, asked wistfully, 'I don't suppose you'd help me look for a suit. You've got such fantastic taste.'

'I'm sorry,' Cleo said quickly, perhaps too quickly, she conceded as Polly's face set in a huffy mask. This latest bombshell made her unfit company for anyone, and the last thing she could settle to do was trail round the shops looking for clothes. She had to contact Jude. 'I really don't have time,' she offered, her grey eyes serious.

Polly shrugged. 'That's OK.'

But she looked brighter when Cleo told her sincerely, 'You don't need me to help you choose what to wear. You always look great.'

* * *

'I'm sorry, Cleo, your husband is tied up in a meeting all afternoon.' Dawn Goodall sounded perky. 'Your husband! You could have knocked me down with the proverbial when I heard you and Mr Mescal were married! I suppose congratulations are in order!'

'Thanks.' Cleo injected warmth into her voice although she felt like howling with frustration. 'How are you coping?'

'Fine,' Dawn laughed lightly. 'I couldn't believe it at first, but he's actually smiled at me a time or two. Marriage has turned him into a human being.'

'I told you you only needed time to get used to him,' Cleo reminded, hating to have to waste time on chit-chat when all she wanted to do was find out from Jude if there was any truth in the takeover rumour.

But the smile slipped from her face as Dawn told her, 'As a matter of fact I was about to phone you. Mr Mescal asked me to let you know he'd be late home this evening. Something suddenly cropped up and he's got a working dinner with some of the consortium who are handling the bid for a chain of American hotels. Just preliminary discussion, you know the sort of thing.'

Cleo did, and if she'd been in the office, functioning in her normal capacity, it would have been she who had arranged the dinner, sat near him, taking it all in, every word, ready to chew over with him later. She would have been the recipient of his innermost cogitations... Instead, she was to dine alone, biting her nails and waiting for him to come home. She didn't know how she managed to end the phone conversation with any civility at all, but she must have done because Dawn sounded unruffled as she said her goodbyes and hung up.

She couldn't believe that Jude would have told her nothing had Mescal Slade been seriously considering a takeover bid for Slade Securities. And why he had to pick this night, of all nights, to be late coming home, she didn't know! It was enough to drive her distracted.

She had kicked her shoes off the moment she'd walked through the front door this afternoon, and now her silk-clad toes curled into the soft pile of the Persian carpet that partially covered the polished oak boards of the study floor as she stared at the phone. She resisted the temptation to call Takeovers and Mergers to fish for the information she needed; she had to speak to Jude about it first.

And there was no question of warning Uncle John. The rumour might be completely unfounded and there was no point in worrying him unnecessarily. Equally, there was no point in speaking to Luke, not until she had the facts. She didn't particularly want to speak to Luke about anything, not after the way he had been this morning, but he was in charge of the company. Her hand hovered over the phone and she bit her lips in indecision before getting up and leaving the room. She would wait for Jude, see what he had to say before alerting any of the family...

She had fallen asleep in front of the drawing-room fire but she snapped to immediate wakefulness when she heard the snick of the door as Jude walked in. He didn't notice her at first, and watching him loosen his tie and run his fingers through his crisp dark hair she thought he looked tired, but when she said, 'Hi—had a good evening?' and uncurled her long legs, standing up, his face lightened, a slow, warm smile curving his long, masculine mouth.

'You shouldn't have waited up.' He came over to her, reaching for her, pulling her close so that their bodies were touching, breast to thigh, the sharp burn of wanting sparking to quick life between them. He bent his dark head, dark hair mingling with soft silver gilt, and he murmured, his mouth finding the taut, slender column of her throat, 'God, you smell good, taste good.'

In a moment, Cleo knew, there would be no question of her mentioning the rumour of the takeover bid. Already the deep need his nearness invoked was claiming her, turning her blood to flame, her mind to mush. So, her hands against the strong wall of his chest, she pushed him away. 'Can I fix you a drink? You look tired.' Her breath was sucked in through her nostrils, making them flare with the sheer effort of clearing her mind, of holding him at bay when all her instincts dictated that she become mindless, melting, a creature created for his pleasure, for the pleasure only he could give her.

'I don't want a drink.' His voice was thick. 'I want you.' He reached for her again but she was too quick for him, her voice rapid and high as she told him,

'I must ask you something.' The smile she slanted in his direction was shaky, because this wasn't what she wanted, not really. She, too, wanted only the wonderful magic that could only be found in his arms, in the depth and delight of their lovemaking.

'Go ahead.'

He slumped in the chair opposite the one she had sunk into and she noticed the tiredness was back in his face, the marks of a man who drove himself too hard. But she owed it to Uncle John, to herself, to find out, so she asked him, 'Is it true that Mescal Slade are considering a takeover of Slade Securities? I heard a rumour.'

'Ah. I think I will have that drink.' He moved over to the drinks tray and Cleo, her eyes on the long male elegance of his back, knew the rumour had solid foundation. And that hurt, more than she had thought possible. Why hadn't he told her? But his features had assumed the poker player's mask that he always used to hide his true feelings when he turned to face her again, and he went to stand in front of the fire, straddle-legged, his glass held in one loosely curved hand.

'So you've heard about the possible takeover bid. It's the good old Chinese Wall syndrome again!' He smiled thinly, rocking back on his heels, his eyes stony. 'The old fiction that each department keeps itself to itself with no gratuitous overlapping of information is a pretty theory, but it hardly ever works.'

'Why didn't you tell me?'

With an effort she kept her voice level, light; she had too much pride to allow him to see her as a whining child, and a cold smile flickered over his mouth as he told her, 'We don't work like that. You, of all people, should know that. You're an interested party.'

'Of course.' Her expression was carefully blank, but she was hurting inside. How could he have kept such a thing from her? She loved him, she was his wife! But, a cold spiteful voice inside her reminded, he didn't love her. As far as he was concerned theirs was an expedient marriage, nothing more. Beyond the bedroom door she was no more to him than she had ever been—one individual among the many employed by Mescal Slade, slightly closer to him than most because of her position as his PA, but that was all.

All at once she needed a drink, too, and she got up stiffly, her body feeling uncoordinated as she moved across the room. When John Slade found out about this it would finish him. He would see all his work, the decision he'd made with her father to break free of Mescal Slade all those years ago, count for nothing.

Her back to Jude, she poured herself a vodka and tonic, trying to control the tremor of her hand, and Jude said quietly, 'There's something else. I think it's time you knew—I'm going to have to find another PA.'

Quite suddenly, the ticking of the pretty grandmother clock seemed louder, the crackle of the logs on the hearth almost deafening. Or maybe it was the silence, the stillness that flooded her brain as she waited for him to explain, that brought everything into sharper focus. So they'd all been right—Polly, Dawn, Sheila Bates—when they'd picked up undercurrents. Jude wanted her out.

She loved her job, didn't want to lose it. Working with Jude made her feel fully alive, it had done since that very first day. And surely he wasn't one of those ghastly old-fashioned men who, clinging to archaic concepts, believed a woman's place was in the home, preferably in chains!

In any case, her chin jutted mutinously, he could fire her—that was his prerogative—but he couldn't stop her going out and finding another job!

He had waited for her to protest, to comment. That much was evident from the arching of one black brow. But Cleo couldn't trust herself to speak, not just yet. And then, as if he could feel her bewilderment, her quick instinctive mutiny, his eyes softened, understanding making them warm as he watched her go back to her chair with the stiff movements of a tautly held body.

'I shall miss you,' he told her quietly. 'Miss your quick mind, your unfailing tact, the flick of dry humour you produce when you want to put me in my place.'

So he had noticed that! And all the time she had imagined she was quietly and unobtrusively manipulating him into making slightly less than impossible demands on himself, on the rest of the staff! And if he would miss her, why then should he fire her? It didn't make sense!

'There are two reasons why I want you to make a move,' he answered the question posed by the puzzled grey eyes. 'In the first place, I don't think it's a particularly good idea for a husband and wife to work so closely together. And secondly, in view of the board's interest in the possibility of a takeover, you'd be far more useful at Slade Securities.'

She hadn't thought of that, but now her mind reluctantly began to follow his.

'Are they in trouble?' Grace had said that her husband had been fretting about the business. Cleo had put that down to his general ill health, but obviously there was more to it than that. And Mescal Slade had started to take a serious interest. Shaky finance houses did well to keep looking over their shoulders, because there were always rock-solid merchant bankers only too ready to swallow them up.

'Some,' Jude replied evenly, shifting, stretching out long, immaculately clad legs, the dark fabric pulled taut across his thighs. 'Since John had to retire, Luke's been overreaching himself. It's a high-risk-capital game, as we know, but recently he's been risking too much—especially in the entrepreneurial section; high flyers with no real and solid grounds for success. The City is getting to know it by now, but if I could persuade the board to back off, forget we ever contemplated a takeover bid, then the other big fishes would have to rethink. If they find out, which I shall make sure they do, that Mescal Slade's interest in Slade Securities has cooled, then they're going to hold off while they sniff the air. You understand?'

She did. She understood, but could do nothing about the game of financial chess Jude was outlining. He had seen her offer of her block of Slade Securities shares as a means of taking personal control of the finance house Mescal Slade were interested in controlling. With her at the helm of the company, no doubt with strong guidance from him, he could become the major shareholder in a newly prosperous concern. Little wonder he'd decided to take up her offer of marriage after she'd told him she'd give him those shares!

'And if you are there,' he leaned forward in his chair, his eyes holding hers intently, 'with your brain, your grasp of what makes the City tick, your financial common sense, then you should have enough time to get Slade Securities back into a position of strength before anyone realises what is happening. Interested?'

'You don't need to ask that,' Cleo replied, her throat tightening. If it were within her power to rescue Slade Securities then she had no choice but to do her damnedest. And that would be what Jude was counting on. The shares she had brought to this marriage would be worth so much more if the company was sound. He was manipulating her, making sure the assets she had brought with her were worth as much as possible. It hurt, like nothing else had hurt before, because in spite of her earlier optimism about the state of their marriage he was no nearer loving her than he had ever been. He was using her. In bed or out of it, he was simply using her.

'When you told me you were firing me I thought it was because you were the type of man who meant to keep his wife at home, looking after the children.' No way was she going to let him know the way she really felt—betrayed, used, as far as ever from having his love. Her role was to be the amenable, totally sensible wife, pulling with him, never against him, never letting him know by word or action how desperately she craved the commitment of his love.

'But I do.' His soft answer left her gasping, but he amended, 'But not quite in the way you imagine. When the children do arrive we'll turn a room here into an office for you, install a computer link-up with Slade's head office, and you can do most of your work from home. No problem. You'll have a nanny, of course, but we'll both make time to be with the children—that's where the house in the country will come in. A place for holidays, weekends, that sort of thing. Fair?'

She nodded, unable to meet his eyes in case he saw the pain there and wondered... Oh, he was being fair, doing everything possible to make their life together a success, and if she didn't love him she might feel the marriage was perfect. But she did love him, more than life, and his calculated manipulation of their future, of the assets she'd brought to this marriage, made her feel cold, cold and lonely.

But she nodded, 'Very fair,' and finished her drink. 'I hope Uncle John and Luke approve our intentions,' she added drily, flinching when he told her,

'I've already consulted them.'

She had been living in a fool's paradise, the last person to know of his intentions. His brain must have been working overtime ever since she'd mentioned those shares in conjunction with her proposal of marriage.

She hardly heard him when he elaborated, 'Your uncle's firmly behind the idea of your joining Slade. So is Luke—but only, I must warn you, because he can't see any way out of the near shambles he's created.'

'Then there seems nothing further to say,' she told him, surprising herself by the equable tone she achieved, and he countered,

'I've often wondered—why didn't you join Slade when you got your degree?'

'Luke.' She shrugged minimally, containing her misery. 'I couldn't stomach the idea of him treating me like a backward junior clerk. Apart from being pompous, he's the type who thinks that being male automatically makes him superior in every degree to a mere female.' And I've discovered that he hates me, which will make working with him almost intolerable, she thought. But Jude wasn't ever going to hear about that, so she added, 'Not to worry, you now own as many shares as he and his father between them, and that, if nothing else, makes me his equal.'

And to her astonishment Jude grinned lazily, stretching, cat-like, in his chair. 'You have a finer mind by far, determination and guts, not to mention all that exquisite packaging. The poor guy's going to have to resign himself to taking a very inferior back seat indeed!'

Almost, she felt flattered. But he was simply seeing her as a brain, a means of pulling Slade Securities—in which, of course, he had a vested interest—together again. He wasn't seeing her as a wife, a woman to be loved.

'I think I'll go up, I'm very tired,' she excused herself, hoping to get out of there before her misery began to show through, and she had reached the door before his voice stopped her, and she turned to see him leave his chair, come over to her.

'You don't mind? It might not seem so from where you're standing, but I don't want to push you into doing something you don't want to do.' The character lines on either side of his mouth indented wryly and he touched the side of her face with a slowly moving finger, his eyes sober. She almost flinched away from his touch because the meaning behind it was shallow. She craved the depths of emotion, not the shallows. But she smiled, shaking her head.

'Of course I don't mind. It's the sensible thing to do.' And she watched his face change, assume the blank poker player's mask again.

That mask always worked well in his business dealings, and had always amused her because she knew how the mind behind the mask was working. But now, when he said, 'And you always do the sensible thing. Quite right, Cleo,' she didn't know whether to take it as a compliment or not. It was one thing to understand how his mind worked in his dealings in the City, quite another to understand his motives, his feelings, in the arena of their marriage.

And that night, for the first time, she pretended to be deeply asleep when he came to their bedroom.

CHAPTER SEVEN

THE last of the everyday cooking utensils and crockery went into a packing case, ready to be taken to Oxfam, and now Cleo had to start wrapping the things of sentimental value—mostly bits and pieces her student friends had given as housewarming presents when she had first moved into the small house in Bow.

These and most of the furniture would go into store. Jude had said, 'You might like to hang on to your things, put them about when we get a place in the country,' and she had agreed, because she had taken time and trouble when furnishing, and some of the pieces were like old and valued friends.

Getting up from her knees, she decided on coffee to help steady her nerves because Robert Fenton had said he'd be here around lunch time, and that could mean anytime between twelve and two.

She tucked the hem of her blue and green striped Viyella shirt back into the waistband of her sleek green needlecord jeans and filled the kettle, plugging it in with hands that shook a little. She would be thankful when today was over, this whole horrible business behind her.

She spooned coffee granules and powdered milk into a mug and waited for the kettle to boil, chewing on a corner of her lower lip. It had seemed a good idea to suggest Fenton collected the money from here. She hadn't wanted him anywhere near the house in Belgravia, but she could have laid down a definite time, an anonymous meeting place—outside some tube station or other.

But she wasn't used to this kind of cloak and dagger stuff, and she hadn't been thinking too clearly when she phoned him yesterday. He would be here anytime during the next two hours. But at least, after then, it would all be over and she could put all her energies into making this marriage work.

But that would be an uphill struggle, she admitted. Those shares had been the primary reason behind his decision to accept her proposal, make her the mother of the children he wanted to have. But she'd always known that, hadn't she? Her conversation with him last night had merely reinforced what she'd already known. Nothing had changed, not really, and besides, she wasn't a quitter and would do everything she could to make this marriage work, and pray that in time love would grow for him, too.

She smiled at this thought, a small, tight smile, and as she poured water into the mug she remembered how she'd sat opposite him at breakfast this morning and he'd asked, 'Are you going to take a look at the Slade Securities books this morning?'

She'd shaken her head, her stomach tying itself in knots because this morning she was collecting the money from the bank, seeing Robert Fenton, and it wasn't a prospect she was over the moon about.

'I'll give him a call and ask him to send all the relevant stuff over in a taxi this afternoon,' she had told him. 'I can work through them in peace here, without him breathing down my neck.'

'Good idea. And don't let him try to put you down.' His mouth quirked humorously. 'Not that I think he could, not in a million years. But just remember, your uncle's on your side all the way, and if you need any help or advice you know you can count on me.'

Jude had finished eating and he'd be leaving for the City soon. Cleo had tried to look on the bright side, because the next time she saw him the nightmare of Robert Fenton would be over and behind her, so she smiled and said, 'Have a good day,'

'Make it a better one?' he'd countered lightly. 'I miss you around the office, so have lunch with me?'

'I'd better not,' she'd said quickly, perhaps too quickly, because she'd caught the slight lift of his brows over cool, enquiring eyes, and she'd just had to explain as she'd followed him to the door, feeling like a worm, 'I thought I'd take myself over to Bow this morning. I need to get things sorted out and packed, and arrange for some of the stuff to go into store. The house agents will be putting the board up next week.'

It had felt like telling lies, although it was part of the truth. And she would phone through and make those arrangements just as soon as Fenton had gone. Until then, she was too edgy to make coherent arrangements with anyone about anything.

It was almost an hour later when the shrill of the doorbell made her drop the pile of books she was moving down from her former bedroom. Her nerves were stretched tight as she stepped over the scattered books, but she took a deep breath and told herself that this would soon be over, and after that she felt calmer, better able to cope.

As she opened the door he was leaning against the frame, smiling unpleasantly; she stepped back and he walked through as if he owned the place.

He was casually dressed and she thought: brown leather trousers, ye gods! and decided they didn't suit him. Neither did the brown silk shirt, open almost to the waist. The outfit marked him as the poseur he was.

Saying nothing, she preceded him to the living-room, untidy now with the bulging cartons and carriers she'd dumped haphazardly because this morning she hadn't been functioning on her normal calm and efficient level. There was a small wall safe behind one of the pictures, installed by a previous owner, and she'd put the package in there as soon as she'd come from the bank. Twenty-five thousand was a lot of money to leave lying around, even for a few hours.

It took a few moments to extract the package, and when she turned he was sprawled out on the sofa, his booted feet on the almond-green upholstery, his eyes avid, following her every movement. He held out his hand wordlessly but she shook her head.

'The hotel receipt first.' She watched coldly as he pulled the scrap of paper from a pocket in his shirt and released it so that it fluttered to the carpet.

'How do you know I haven't had it photocopied?' he asked, his face blank, and she snapped,

'You probably have. But I'd advise you not to try it on again. Just pay off your debts and stay away from me.' She tossed the package at him, disgust on her face. 'Now get out!'

He turned his head, staring at her, his face tightening. 'You weren't always so keen to see the back of me.'

'I didn't know what a creep you were then,' she grated, her control precarious now. She couldn't bear to be reminded that she had once found him remotely likeable. It made her feel ashamed to know that she had ever been so blind, so gullible. And he knew that, he'd have to be a fool not to, and his mouth whitened with temper as he retaliated,

'But *I* knew what a pain *you* were! My God—when I think of the time I put in—all those boring trips to the country, the ghastly picnics, the cosy meals you dished up here and the predictable, prissy "hands off" signals if I did more than kiss you! God, what a bore it all was. And for what? For sweet damn-all!'

He tipped the contents of the package on the sofa, swinging his legs to the floor, his eyes furious. 'I reckon you owe me this! You can't actually imagine I enjoyed sucking up to you, listening to you boring on about your wretched exam results and then your precious career? So, having said that, and put the record straight,' his voice changed, was smooth as oil, 'you don't mind if I count this, I hope. Not being trustworthy myself, I don't trust anyone else. Not even a self-righteous prude like you.'

So she gritted her teeth, not bothering to tell him to be quick about it, because even saying that would waste precious seconds and she wanted him out of here. He tainted the air. And when he had finished he stood up, looking down at the piles of notes—tens and twenties— spread out on the almond-green fabric.

'I should have asked for double,' he said.

'Just take it and go,' she gritted, controlling her voice with difficulty because she felt like screaming.

He raised his head then, tearing his eyes from the small fortune spread out in front of him, and he looked at her, at the taut whiplash lines of her body, and his eyes held something unspeakable.

'You always were a frigid bitch,' he mouthed slowly, and then advanced, putting himself between her and the door. 'But you're a married bitch now, and maybe Mescal's taught you what it's all about.'

He began to circle her and she sidestepped, her heart beginning to race, and she realised when it was too late to do anything about it that he had manoeuvred her into a corner.

'Don't come near me!' Her eyes glittered with a mixture of rage and fear, and he said thickly,

'Why not? I'll show you what you missed that night in Goldingstan.'

He made a single swift movement, lunging for her, but she twisted out of his reach, his hands finding nothing more substantial than the cloth of her shirt, and the buttons ripped as she jerked frenziedly away, the fabric parting to reveal the rounded globes of her breasts, barely covered by the midnight-blue lace of her scantily cut bra.

There was no time to think about making herself decent again, she had to get out of here because Fenton was serious, deadly serious, his hot eyes on her exposed skin. She made a desperate attempt to reach the door, but he was quick—and fitter than he deserved to be, considering his life-style—and he caught her, bringing her down in a fair imitation of a rugby tackle, knocking the breath out of her lungs as his body fell on hers.

Cleo twisted and fought, but he caught her head between his hands, twisting until she thought her hair would come out by the roots, and she began to scream, but he silenced her with his savage mouth and blood thundered in her head, a pounding roar. But she heard, above it, a voice like perma-frost.

'Just what the hell is going on?'

And then there was silence, and stillness, like the eye of a storm. Fenton's body went rigid on top of hers, and the taste of fear was on his lips which were still clamped over her mouth.

Then all was violence, movement and noise as Fenton's body was dragged from her, the sound of ripping fabric, the tearing of brown silk as Jude hauled him to his feet, flinging him against the wall.

Cleo opened her eyes, relief at Jude's timely arrival warring with panic as his glittering eyes swept over her sprawled body, her near-naked breasts, her wildly tangled hair. And his eyes held murder, dark, icy murder.

She tried to tell him it wasn't what it seemed, that she had not been a willing partner in that torrid embrace, that he had saved her from possible rape, but the sounds she made were thickly incoherent and he turned from her as though she sickened him and she saw the lean, strong hands curl into fists as he swung round to tell Fenton, 'Get out before I tear you apart.'

Fenton hauled himself together as Cleo scrambled to her feet, tugging the two halves of her ripped shirt together, her breath coming raggedly. The younger man wasn't leaving without taking what he had come for, but Cleo saw how his hands shook as he tucked his shirt back into his tight leather trousers.

Jude's face was set, the darkly tanned skin pulled tight over jutting bones, danger explicit in every line of his athletically powerful body, so Cleo had to give Fenton a grudging ten marks for courage as he sauntered over to the sofa and began to pick up the piles of notes.

'On my way, mate,' he drawled. 'But I can't leave without taking my little gift, can I? Might hurt the lady's feelings.'

'Did you give him that?' Jude's eyes flicked coldly to her then back to Fenton, and the harsh, incisive tone made her blood run cold.

'Yes.' There was no point in lying, no point at all, and she felt giddy, the room swaying, and she wished she could faint because she'd rather be unconscious, in a coma, than have to try to explain all this away.

She closed her eyes briefly, fighting rising nausea, and she didn't see what happened next but she heard Jude's voice, dark and deadly, 'Get out. Now, before I plaster the wall with you.' And no one who wasn't a suicidal idiot would ignore that kind of menace, because it filled the small room, turning the air sharp with violence, and she dragged her eyes open to see Fenton scurrying out.

He had left the money behind, and Jude grated, 'Pick it up.'

He looked as if he hated her, as if the very sight of her disgusted him, and she stared at him with huge grey frightened eyes, her body shaking, perspiring—although she felt very cold.

The evidence he had walked in on was damning in itself; the money she'd admitted she'd given Robert Fenton made everything worse. She was going to have to tell him the truth about the way she'd been blackmailed, explain that she'd rather part with a slice of her inheritance than bring shame and embarrassment—and possibly something much worse—on to the sick old man who had been the only person she had ever received anything remotely like affection from during the past ten years.

Agitation made her voice shake as she took a tentative step towards him, her hands outspread in involuntary supplication.

'Jude—let me explain.'

'Just do as I said,' his voice lashed her. 'Pick that stuff up. And don't say anything, not a word, otherwise I might forget you're a female.'

He wouldn't listen, not now, not in this mood. She dragged herself to the sofa and dropped to her knees, her fingers shaking as she began to push the piled notes together in a bunch. He didn't consider that anything she could say could explain or justify the situation he had walked in on. He couldn't trust her. But then, he didn't love her, so why should he?

From the corner of her eyes she saw him move, bend to pick up a scrap of paper from the floor, and his voice was iced over with contempt as he crumpled the hotel receipt and dropped it to the floor again.

'A souvenir, I take it. Been reliving old times, have you? God, he must have something if the affair's been going on that long!' His mouth curled bitterly and she had never seen his eyes so cold. 'So why didn't you marry him to gain access to the money you obviously intend to pour all over him? And don't bother to answer, let me tell you! Because there was no way your guardians would have approved your marriage to him—and so your considerable financial assets would have been frozen for another year. Tough on him, that. He likes to spend, I take it!' His mouth thinned, displaying a cruelty she hadn't seen before. 'Was he getting restive, threatening to move to greener pastures? Was that why you hatched a plan to marry someone your guardians *would* approve of? And so, as I heard him saying when you'd invited him to my house, two days after becoming my wife, in order to get your hands on one fortune, you married another. Mine. Sweet heaven—did you imagine I'd sit by and let you lavish mine on him once you'd run through yours?'

Things were going from bad to worse, and she couldn't bear it because what he was saying, accusing her of, was nothing like the truth. And now, if ever, was the time to make him see that. She was crazily in love with him and she wanted him to love her, and if she couldn't put the record straight then this morning's débâcle would put the possibility of that ever happening back a hundred years.

She scrambled to her feet, the notes pushed all anyhow back in the package, and he held a hand out, wordlessly, his eyes midnight ice as they swept dismissively over her.

'It isn't what you think,' she began, her courage almost deserting her under that cruelly denigrating look.

'Save your breath,' he cut in tonelessly. 'The scene I walked in on was explicit enough, and the hotel receipt confirms that you had no intention of losing a lover of some long-standing.' His hard eyes impaled her, making her feel ill. 'He must be sensational in bed. So much so that you couldn't stand the deprivation. That's why you asked me to make love to you on the island. Any port in a storm.'

'No!' Appalled, she put a hand to her mouth to stop the words from tumbling out. She had asked him to make love to her because she had just realised how much she loved him. But he wouldn't believe that, not now, and if she tried to make him believe it he would end up despising her even more because he'd think she was trying to wheedle her way round him!

'No?' A black brow arched disbelievingly. 'I can't think of any other reason. And I've no intention of listening to any fairy story you might try to invent.' He tossed the package around in his hands, as if trying to evaluate the exact amount. 'I'll pay this back into your account. You are free to do as you like with your own money,' he commented savagely, 'except to give massive handouts to your lover. Like it or not, you are my wife, and, as my wife, I expect certain standards of behaviour.'

He turned from her dismissively, staring out of the small paned window. 'Get your coat. I'm taking you home. And don't ever think of trying to see that jerk again or I'll keep you under lock and key.'

Staring at the rigid line of his shoulders, the arrogant tilt of his head, a hot tide of pure rage flooded through her, burning her up, and she turned on her heels to fetch her jacket from the kitchen, her voice shaking with anger as she spat over her shoulder,

'Who the hell do you think you are? God? Well, I hope you find the judgement throne comfortable—although it's probably too small for your massive ego!'

She wasn't waiting for any reply, and she wasn't even going to try to tell him the truth! He had sat in judgement, condemning her, without hearing her side of the story, saying things, horrible things, things that cheapened the love she had felt for him, the ecstasy she had found in his arms. And she had her pride; she wouldn't go down on her knees and beg!

But the heated rush of anger fell away, draining her, and her eyes filled with scalding tears as she saw the carton he must have dropped on the table near the door as he'd walked in and found his wife sprawled out on the floor, another man's body covering her, another man's mouth on hers.

The name of the local delicatessen was plainly printed across the carton in bright yellow letters, so the contents were a foregone conclusion. And there was no mistaking the bottle of Moselle for what it was, either. He'd asked her to have lunch with him, to make his day better, and she'd told him she'd be here, working, and so he had come to her, bringing their lunch, because he'd rather picnic with her than eat off the best china in the most exclusive restaurant in town. And if he hadn't walked in and found her with Fenton then she would have been the happiest woman alive because his action, even if he hadn't realised it, meant that she was at last beginning to mean something to him.

But now he thought her to be a two-timing slut, and the hopes she'd had of their marriage developing into a two-way, long-term love-affair were dead as cold ashes. And no sadness could be as great as this.

CHAPTER EIGHT

'CLEO?' Dawn's voice came brightly over the wire. 'I've just had a call from Mr Mescal. He asked me to get you to have Thornwood meet him at the airport at five-thirty, and to remind you the Blairs are expected tonight. OK?'

'Thanks, Dawn. I'll pass the message to Thornwood right away.' She was about to ring off, feeling herself colour as she realised that Dawn just had to be wondering why Jude had phoned her and not his wife, but Dawn chattered on, 'How's the new job going? I must say I miss you here. And couldn't you have persuaded your husband not to promote that Sheila Bates to your old job? Nobody likes her, I'm told, so I'm sure I won't.'

As Dawn seemed set to gossip for hours, Cleo cut in smoothly, advising, 'I'm sure she'll be fine, just get on with your job and leave her to get on with hers. Lovely to talk to you, but I must dash—Jude wants to make an impression on Sir Geoffrey this evening.'

Which was as good an excuse as any to cut the conversation short, even though Meg had everything in hand for this evening and there wasn't a thing Cleo had to do apart from dress herself up and dredge up a smile and a line in relaxed conversation from somewhere. She didn't feel in the mood to talk to anyone, not even Dawn. She was so tense she felt she might explode, disintegrate into a million ragged pieces.

On Tuesday morning, after discovering her with Fenton, Jude had driven her home in a stinging silence and had departed, almost immediately, for Zurich. And late this afternoon he would be back, and before the

Blairs arrived for dinner she was going to have to make him listen to her explanations.

He had been too angry to listen to anything she could have said the last time she had seen him, and she could understand that, but today he simply had to hear her side of the story. The sordid business about Fenton's blackmailing threats would have to be exposed and, in a way, it would be a relief because Jude might be able to help.

Her hands shook as she pushed together the pile of papers, the reports and balance sheets she'd been ploughing through, and slid them into an empty drawer in the desk in Jude's study. It hadn't taken her long to realise that Slade Securities was in a mess, and she couldn't begin to see a way out while her mind was in such turmoil. Loving Jude as she did, his disgust with her, the loathing she'd seen in those cold, azure eyes, was a constant and debilitating pain, blinding her to everything else.

And her worries about Fenton's possible next move didn't help any, she acknowledged as she pushed herself listlessly to her feet on her way to find Thornwood and relay Jude's message. Fenton hadn't had the money he'd demanded, so heaven only knew what his next move would be. She didn't know whether to expect a renewed demand or to see, in print, the whole sordid pack of lies. And if that happened she couldn't bear to think what would happen to Uncle John. And Luke, for one, would make sure the old man read every word.

It was like living with a time bomb. But maybe, when Jude knew the truth, he would know what to do.

'You certainly know how to make yourself look sexy, but then you've had plenty of practice, for Fenton, haven't you?'

Cleo twisted round, her heart pumping wildly. Wearing her new dress, she had been putting the finishing touches to her make-up when he'd walked in on her.

She hadn't heard the bedroom door open and now he was leaning against the frame. He looked tired, world-weary, the lines of cynicism deeply scored beside his mouth. Disadvantaged, she looked at him with anguished eyes, the smoke-grey irises deepened to charcoal. She had planned on being ready when he returned, composed, waiting in the drawing-room. But Thornwood must have had a smoother drive from the airport than she had bargained for and her fingers froze, dropping the scent spray she'd been using on to the polished rosewood surface of the dressing-table. The tiny clatter broke the silence of his long, unwavering scrutiny and she said, 'We have to talk,' and tried to get herself together. He had to listen to her. He had to. She would never get through this evening if he didn't.

'Must we?' His tone was bored as he moved slowly into the room, loosening his tie, and her heart jumped, but she resisted the impulse to run. She wasn't a coward, although his patent disgust with her, his terrifying coldness, wasn't making things easy.

'Yes, we must.' She was ashamed of the slight tremor in her voice, of the hunger she was sure must show in her eyes as she watched him remove his suit jacket, his hands moving next to the zip of his trousers. God, but he was superb, almost frighteningly male, and he was her husband, and she loved him, and he loathed her!

But she was about to change all that, wasn't she? Because after she'd explained about Fenton he would go back to being the caring, exciting lover and beloved companion he had been before, surely he would? She knew he had been on the verge of growing more than fond of her. She couldn't believe that wasn't true, and she had to cling on to that.

He was naked now and she closed her eyes against a sudden inrush of pain, of need, that gripped her like a giant steel hand. She had to get him to listen, to understand.

'Jude——'

'Don't you think you ought to go down?' The look he flicked in her direction might have been given to an irritating child. 'Sir Geoffrey and his wife will be here in an hour. You should be checking with Meg.'

He didn't pause in his progress towards the bathroom, and that, and the irritated look, riled her. She wasn't so completely besotted by love that she would allow him to brush her aside like a subnormal hireling!

'This won't take long.' Resolve stiffened her spine as she moved between him and the adjoining bathroom door, her chin lifting defiantly, her eyes unwavering even as she faced the exasperated lowering of his black brows. 'You've judged and condemned me without a hearing, and I deserve better than that!'

'You deserve a thrashing.' His mouth twisted down in a sneer. 'But I'm too much a gentleman to give it to you! But I tell you this——' He moved closer, and his tanned, taut nakedness seared her through the filmy fabric of her dress, making her shudder at the awareness of how easily he could rouse her, even in his hatred. He didn't touch her, he didn't need to, and her words of hot protest at his high-handed refusal even to listen to her side of the story died in her throat, clogging it. 'I know now why you married me. I didn't have to be a genius to work that out,' he flared, controlled anger making his eyes glitter. 'You needed to get your hands on your inheritance and you couldn't afford to wait another twelve months because your lover was getting restive. He wanted to get his hands on that so-called little gift he was practically drooling over. And you couldn't marry him to gain access to your inheritance, no matter how much you might have wanted to, because there's no way your guardians would have approved a jerk like him. So you married me, and, OK——' his breath sucked harshly into his lungs, making the rough satin of his skin quiver with an inner tension she could feel through every fibre of her being, as if he were an extension of herself '—so now I know, and, granted, our marriage was only ever one of expediency—but you're still my wife.'

Suddenly, his hands were at her throat, making her heart flutter in panic as the balls of his thumbs, beneath her chin, forced her head back, forced her to read the dark intent in his eyes.

'You will not be seeing Fenton again, and as that means you'll be deprived of the pleasures of his bed and his body, I've decided to help you.' His voice lowered to the threatening purr of a tiger and she shuddered helplessly, cold with the chill of the hating mockery that was looking at her from those narrowed, glittering eyes. 'You are one hell of a highly sexed lady, as I found out when you begged me to make love to you, when you used me to satisfy your needs in Fenton's absence. So, just to help you,' his mouth curled derisively, 'I'll make love to you until you're reeling. I'll make damned sure you know who you belong to, and you won't have enough strength left to even *think* of Fenton!'

He released her suddenly. And shaken, appalled, by what she was hearing she registered his voice, coming as if from a misty distance.

'Now get downstairs and see if Meg needs any help. Start earning your keep!'

* * *

Meeting Jude's sardonic eyes across the table Cleo thought, *I hate him! Hate him!*, then inclined her head to listen to what Sir Geoffrey was saying.

He was a short, round man who loved his food—as evidenced by the way he had relished the saddle of lamb and was now enjoying a second helping of syllabub. No doubt he would make hearty inroads into the cheeseboard, Cleo decided, thus prolonging the agony of having to sit opposite Jude with his sardonic eyes and derisive endearments. But at least Sir Geoffrey's appetite made up for her lack of one, although Jude would have noticed, she conceded edgily, picking up her wineglass and drinking recklessly. He had hardly taken his eyes from her throughout the meal. It was a subtle form of torture.

Whenever she had glanced up at the cold, hard, self-righteous devil, she had found him watching her with those clever, knowing, shaming eyes. And her skin had crawled with hot colour as she'd recalled his threat to make love to her until she reeled—and why. And so she had looked his way as little as possible, putting her mind to conversing with Sir Geoffrey and Hilda, his scrawny, overdressed wife.

Neither of them would know that things were very far from perfect between the handsome, urbanely charming chief executive of Mescal Slade and his new wife. They wouldn't be able to read behind the cynicism of his superficial smiles, those lying words of endearment, to the utter contempt he felt for her.

So much for her stupid belief that she only had to talk rationally to him to make him listen to her because he, more than anyone else she knew, was rational to his fingertips. And how could she have ever believed she could make things right between them again? Her arrogant husband had made up his mind. As far as he was concerned she was devious, sly, unfaithful and greedy, and that was that. No amount of pleading or explaining on her part would make him change his mind.

And so she wouldn't demean herself by pleading for a fair hearing ever again!

Unguardedly, she caught his eyes again, saw the hateful, mocking gleam as he answered a gushing request Lady Blair had just lobbed into the air.

'I'm sure Cleo will let you have the recipe for the syllabub, Hilda. Won't you, my darling?' And, expounding hatefully, his long strong fingers toying idly with his silver fruit knife, his smile holding a savagery only Cleo could detect, 'I'm fortunate in having such a devotedly domesticated wife. She, I'm delighted to say, neglects no area of my—comfort.'

'Such a beautiful wife, too,' Sir Geoffrey chimed in gallantly, and Cleo felt her face burn with rage because domesticated she was not, and Jude knew it, and his reference to 'comfort' had an entirely different connotation.

Hoping the Blairs would attribute her fiery colour to new-bride embarrassment over Jude's seeming compliment, she plastered a smile on her face.

'I'll ask Meg for the recipe, of course. Now, shall we have coffee in the drawing-room, Hilda? Leave the men to what will probably be interminable business talk.'

Thankfully, Hilda was a talkative lady and Cleo only needed to make smiling responses now and again, so she should have been able to relax, but she didn't. Sooner or later their guests would leave. And then what? Would Jude walk away from her with icy contempt, or would he make good his threat to make love to her until she couldn't even think? Both options made her feel physically ill. She didn't want to be alone with him.

Almost hysterically, she wondered what Sir Geoffrey and his wife would say if she begged them to stay for the night—for the rest of the week, for the rest of the month!

Curbing the impulse to stride around the room, pulling her hair out by the handful, she injected what she prayed were the right noises into Hilda's non-stop chatter and almost leapt out of her skin when the door opened and Jude brought Sir Geoffrey through.

The tubby little man looked pleased with life, rubbing his hands together, his smile effusive, and from that, and Jude's look of grim satisfaction, Cleo deduced that Jude had won the Blair and Dowd account, which was what he'd been angling for.

It wasn't long before their guests left and the house was silent, the only sound Cleo was aware of was her own shallow breathing. And she scrambled to her feet as Jude came back into the drawing-room, closing the door behind him, leaning against it as he untied his tie, his eyes never leaving her face.

'How much have you been able to gather from the Slade Securities books? I take it you made a start on them while I was away?'

About to tell him she was on her way to bed—the frosty words on the edge of her tongue—she stared right back at him, her heart jerking. Did he have to be so cold, so unforgiving? Not that there was actually anything to forgive, but he wouldn't believe that in a million years.

If only, a desperate little voice in her mind nudged, if only they could start conversing normally again, together about something in which they shared a common interest, then maybe she could find a way through to him and force him to accept he'd been wrong about her.

'As far as I've been able to tell, it's looking pretty groggy.'

She forced a level tone, forced herself to return to a chair. She had to stay calm. This wasn't personal, this was business, and they were perfectly attuned on that level, she had to remember that. But could she hold her own, given the churning state of her emotions? She doubted even that when he shot, smooth as ice, 'And?'

Her eyes clouded, and her hands felt clammy. He clearly expected her to have some idea of how to remedy the situation, and he was short on patience. But she hadn't been able to bring her usual concentration to the project—how could she, when her equilibrium had been shattered by what had happened? Not to mention her worries about what Robert Fenton might decide to do next!

'I'm waiting to hear your conclusions.' He had removed his tie now, his jacket, and the whiteness of his shirt contrasted starkly with the depth of his tan, his crisp, dark hair, the close-fitting black trousers that skimmed long, lean legs. He was standing, a brandy-glass in his hand, but although he was still there was a restlessness in him she could feel, an intimation of tension in the way he held his head.

'I honestly don't know.' She was on the defensive now. 'I haven't begun to form any conclusions. I've had too much on my mind,' she qualified with a bitterness she couldn't hide.

'Like Fenton?' he came back immediately, his mouth tightening, and Cleo felt drained and hopeless, her face paper-white. What was the use? What *was* the use?

'No, not Fenton,' she told him wearily, and felt her head begin to ache. It wasn't the strict truth, of course. Fenton had been on her mind, but not for the reasons Jude persisted in believing.

And her depression deepened when he stated flatly, 'I don't believe you. But you're going to have to root him out of your mind and start concentrating on how to pull Slade Securities out of the mire. After all,' he slammed his empty glass down on the drinks table, making her flinch with the leashed violence of the action, 'I've a sizeable interest in the company now—you signed your shares over to me as a payment for the right to get your hands on enough ready cash to satisfy your lover, remember? So when you've come up with a few ideas, let me know, and we'll discuss them.' He picked up his suit jacket and hooked it over his shoulder. 'I'm going to bed now, and I suggest you do, too.' He paused at the door, his voice cutting, 'I don't need to remind you that those shares were only a down payment for my services as your husband. And I intend to extract what's owing. With interest.'

He closed the door quietly behind him and she stared at its blank surface mutinously. There was no way she was going to climb into the huge bed they had shared since returning from their honeymoon. No way on God's sweet earth! Tight with rage, she paced the room, pouring herself a generous dose of brandy and swallowing it recklessly.

She was seeing a side of him she hadn't known existed. She had always admired his objectivity, his ability to see all sides of a given situation, a given problem, his careful weighing of every angle. But in this situation he was seeing only the side he wanted to see, refusing to admit there could be another. And that wasn't like the man she had come to know, like and respect. He was acting out of character, being deliberately cruel, and his treatment of her was an insult.

Every time he killed her attempts to tell him the truth he insulted her. And if he thought she was going to share his bed then he had to be out of his mind! And if she had any sense at all she would walk out on him now and never come back. And he could whistle for what he thought she owed him!

But walking out would point to her guilt—in his jaundiced eyes, it would! He would believe she had gone to Fenton. And besides, she admitted drearily, she still loved him, believed, crazily, that there was still a chance for them. Somewhere.

But tonight she wouldn't sleep with him.

There was a slip of a dressing-room adjoining the master bedroom and it contained a narrow bed. Jude had used it for the first two nights after their wedding because she had stipulated they wouldn't sleep together for the first two weeks of their marriage.

He had respected her wishes, for some reason choosing to use the tiny room rather than the far more comfortable guest-room. And she had admired him for that, for the way he had obviously wanted to spare her any puzzled looks she might have received from Meg. He had been a different man then, she thought miserably as she made her way reluctantly upstairs. He was a frightening stranger now.

She couldn't use the dressing-room, of course, so Meg would have to draw her own conclusions. Because even if Jude were already asleep, which she doubted, he would hear her and wake no matter how quietly she moved across the bedroom. But she had to sleep somewhere and the guest-room was the only other choice, because she wasn't sleeping with him. She had too much pride to share intimacy with a man who hated and despised her, even if he was her husband.

The bed in the guest-room was always kept made up and aired, and the room itself was only slightly less luxurious than the one she and Jude had shared until now. But she wasn't interested in her surroundings, and a sob built up in her throat, hurting, as she unzipped her dress and reflected that her marriage, which had once seemed to hold so much promise, was dead before it had properly come alive.

Clad only in a pair of midnight-blue satin briefs and tiny matching bra, she pulled back the bedcovers and viewed the cool linen sheets with less than enthusiasm.

'I prefer our bed,' Jude said, from right behind her, and before she knew what was happening he had scooped her up into his arms and her eyes widened with shock, for one still second, before she realised exactly what was happening and began to pummel her fists against his naked chest.

'What the hell do you think you're doing?' she spat, burningly, shamingly aware of his near nakedness, and hers. He was wearing only silky pyjama bottoms, and her scantily covered breasts were pressed against the warm satin of his skin. And, shamingly, a sheet of heated sensation flooded her body at the contact and she grew still, her body painfully rigid as she tried to hold herself away from him.

Her breath caught in her throat, a dry, painful sob, as he carried her out of the room. She would not be manhandled this way, but her renewed struggles had no effect at all on his effortless stride as he carried her along the dimly lit corridor to their own room.

'I'm taking you to my bed, where you belong,' he answered her angry question tersely. 'Scream if you like. The Thornwoods are safely tucked up in their quarters at the rear of the house. I doubt if they'd hear if you blew a trumpet.'

Pushing the bedroom door shut behind him with his foot, he crossed the pale ochre wool of the carpet in three long strides, dropping her to the smooth olive green cover of the bed and was down on top of her, his hips pinning her to the mattress, before she could move.

'This will be rape,' she warned throatily, her eyes glittering feverishly between the tumbled strands of her silkily silver hair, her breath coming quickly, making the rounded peaks of her breasts rise and fall rapidly.

'I don't think so.' He captured her clenched and flailing hands in one of his and shifted slightly, making her aware of his arousal, and she moaned, low in her throat, just once, as his lips descended to take hers.

Desperately, she clamped her mouth shut, trying to ignore the fever of need he was already arousing within her as his tongue forced her lips apart. But, as she had unconsciously known he would, he won that battle and she capitulated weakly to the insistent pressure of his mouth. And then, as if he knew he had her subdued, mindless, he trailed moist kisses down the length of her throat and on and down to circle her breasts, tormenting the aroused peaks until she could have screamed her frustration, her unwilling yet insistent need.

Then, gently, he eased the fabric of her bra aside, revealing first one tautly inviting breast and then the other, and she writhed frantically beneath him, moaning her rejection of the way he made her feel.

He had warned her that he would make love to her until she couldn't think straight, and this was precisely what he was doing.

Before, when they had made love, she had welcomed him eagerly, lovingly, knowing that at least he cared for her, that he found her body and her wanton response to him exciting. But this was something else, and, as he bent his dark head to suckle on the rosy-peaked breasts her traitorous body offered in open invitation, she made one last feeble attempt to stop him.

'Leave me alone!' It was a plea, a muted cry of despair, and she heard a rough echo of that despair in his voice as he derided,

'I would if I damned well could!'

And his mouth closed over one taut nipple, sucking moistly, making blind desire kick to urgent life inside her and she was lost in the devastating sensation of his hands, his mouth, his body, as he kissed and fondled every inch of her silky, sweat-slicked skin until she was ready to beg him to take her.

And then, poised above her accepting body, his face flushed with the dark blood of desire, he held her thrashing head in his hands, held it still so that she had no option but to meet the blaze of triumph in his eyes as his potent maleness tantalisingly nudged her ardent, feminine moistness.

'Who am I?' Vivid blue eyes froze her soul yet seared her senses, and her body grew still, waiting, tormented, uncomprehending.

'Do you know who I am, what I am?' he insisted, and she closed her eyes, her body aching for the relief only he could bring, the relief he was withholding. He was playing games with her, and she shuddered hopelessly as his voice ground out, 'Open your eyes, damn you! Look at me. I'm not Fenton, so don't even try to pretend I am! I'm your husband, the man who is going to make love to you, again and again, until you don't know who you are or what you are, until all you can know, feel, taste, think, is me!'

And then he took her, almost savagely, as if he would never have enough of her, as time and time again he forced her to the delirious heights of shaming ecstasy.

CHAPTER NINE

CLEO tried to make her mind focus on what she was doing as she neared the bottom of the escalator. Stepping off, she took a firmer grip on her briefcase and was swept along with the tide of home-bound commuters. The Underground in the rush-hour was hell. But then, wasn't everything, these days?

This afternoon, spent with Luke in his office, had been grim. He'd made no effort to hide his dislike. And in her heightened emotional state it had been difficult to take. But she'd managed, though heaven only knew how, ignoring his scathing, 'Wonder Woman to the rescue!' as he'd scanned her outlined proposals for the salvaging of Slade Securities.

'Jude's approved this, I take it?' He'd finally laid the papers aside. 'Or is the whole proposal his brainchild?'

His derisive look had told her that, no matter what she said, he'd would never believe a mere female could come up with such precise figures and projections. He couldn't believe it because it would damage his ego. As far as he was concerned, only a masculine mind was capable of a clear-sighted and logical grasp of finance.

She hadn't disabused him; there had seemed no point. No point in anything these days. And she didn't have the emotional resources to endure a ding-dong verbal fight with him. Jude had drained her emotions dry.

Far from consulting Jude, she had said nothing about the conclusions she'd formed after days and days of concentrated work. True, he had asked her to let him know her findings, so that they could discuss them, and that was because he had a vested interest now. But the salvation of Slade Securities while it was still salvageable was her baby. She owed it to Uncle John. The fact that Jude now had thirty per cent of the voting stock was neither here nor there. She wasn't doing it for him. How could she willingly do anything for him when he persisted in treating her like dirt?

'Cleo?' A hand touched her shoulder and she twisted round, her racing heart a testimony to how edgy she had become over the past ten days, quieting down to normal as she encountered Dawn's puzzled eyes.

'I thought it was you,' Jude's secretary explained. 'Though I couldn't be absolutely sure. You look awful. Lost weight, haven't you?' On that unflattering note Dawn prepared for a natter session, oblivious to the grim-faced throngs pushing past in their rush to squeeze on to homebound trains.

'I've been working flat out.' Cleo put on a brightish smile and lifted one shoulder in a gesture she hoped denoted unconcern. 'You know how it is—too busy to eat properly. Anyway,' she turned the subject quickly, 'how's Sheila settling down in my old job?' Dawn was far from a fool and Cleo didn't want anyone to guess that everything had turned sour between Jude and herself.

Dawn pulled a face. 'So-so. I couldn't stand her at first. She's capable enough but hell—those damned airs and graces. She acted as if she expected me to drop a curtsey every time she walked by.' She grinned suddenly, wryly. 'But we started to gel after that husband of yours reduced her to tears yesterday. I knew exactly how she felt! It's a pity you ever left. You were the only one who could handle him, make him remotely human. He's been worse than ever this last week or so. A real s.o.b., if you don't mind my saying so! And if he doesn't change his tune I, for one, am definitely looking for another job.' Then a doubtful look flickered over her middle-aged face, as if she was afraid she'd said too much. 'I still think of you more as being his PA than as his wife. So excuse my big mouth, but you might do some good if you dropped a word in his ear.'

'I'll see what I can do,' Cleo said. Dawn had her sympathy, but she knew Jude would not listen to what she had to say on that, or any other subject. He would be more likely to walk naked through the centre of London in the rush-hour! And that made her recall the time when he would have made a point of listening to anything she had to say because in those days he had respected her viewpoint, her intelligence. There was nothing he respected about her now. She didn't even respect herself. And the knowledge hurt, filled her chest with pain. Quickly, before Dawn could guess her misery, she excused, 'I have to go, Dawn. Sorry to rush off, but I'm late as it is. And keep your chin up—try to remember, his bark's worse than his bite. And stand up to him if you think he's out of line.'

Not very helpful advice, she guessed, as Dawn's shoulders lifted in a helpless shrug beneath her sedate dark green coat. Cleo didn't want Jude's staff deserting him. She cared about him, still loved him, despite the way he'd been treating her, despite knowing, now, that he would never return her love.

Fenton, and Jude's reaction to the situation—as he stubbornly perceived it—had killed whatever chance their marriage might once have had. And as for that louse, Fenton, there hadn't been a peep out of him since Jude had ordered him out of the house in Bow. Maybe Jude's ferocity had made him think twice about carrying out his threats.

* * *

Her feet dragged as she emerged from the tube station at Knightsbridge. It was raining now, the heavy drizzle wetting her charcoal silk suit. It hung on her body where once—before her ill-fated marriage to Jude—it had clung lovingly.

Reluctant to return to the cold comfort of the luxurious Regency house in Belgravia, she lingered in the almost deserted streets, growing colder, wetter, until an opulent saloon swept by, spraying her with muddy rainwater before purring on, its tail-lights glittering in the murk, her existence of no more importance than that of a fallen leaf.

Wiping ineffectually at the mud stains that had probably ruined the suit for ever, the first stirrings of rebellion stirred to life. She was sick to death of being made to feel that her existence was of no importance whatever. Her cousin hated her for some warped reason of his own and her husband didn't give a damn so long as she was an available body in his bed. A body he could use and punish.

She wasn't going to stand for it any longer!

She doubled her pace, her high heels beating a determined tattoo on the wet pavements, her shoulders straight. She still loved Jude but she wasn't going to allow him to make her feel defeated, shabby, worthless. Nor would she allow him to use her body to wreak his own savage brand of vengeance. He gave her no quarter. He made love to her with an eroticism that shamed her when, in the clear light of morning, she recalled the depths of response he was so easily able to draw from her. Somehow, she was going to regain her self-respect!

His lovemaking was a bitter travesty of what they had shared earlier on in their marriage. Erotic it might be, but it was also a method of marking her as his possession, murdering her pride, making her hate herself for her uninhibited and ungovernable response.

Not any more, though. If there were to be any hope for the future of their marriage at all then it would have to be in name only until their differences were resolved—if they ever could be. She would use the guestroom, or move out altogether, and to hell with his objections, because the sort of marriage they had at this moment wasn't worth a damn.

Despite the now drenching rain, her neat pointed chin was set at a grimly determined angle as she ran up the four shallow steps that led to the front door and hunted through her handbag for her key. But the door swung open before her chilled fingers had located the key and Jude snapped, 'Where the hell have you been?'

A frisson of distaste snaked through her and her mouth compressed to a tight line as she pushed past him into the hall. Let him rage if he wanted—she was about to show him she had a mind of her own and would not be treated like worthless garbage!

The old Cleo was back, her fighting spirit stronger than ever after its absence during the last ten days.

'To discuss the future of Slade Securities with Luke,' she answered him tartly, then swung past him. 'Excuse me, I have to get out of these wet things.'

But he caught her, pulling her round, and there was nothing gentle about his grip as hard fingers bit into the fragile bones of her shoulders.

'Luke?' he queried nastily, his eyes narrow azure slits. 'Or was it Fenton?'

Cleo drew in a tired breath, striving to hold on to her new determination to hold her own. 'Luke,' she emphasised stonily, shuddering inside as his fingers bit more deeply. 'And if you don't believe me——'

'Why should I believe anything you say——' he interrupted cuttingly, 'when I walked in on a truth that turned everything you'd ever said or done into a living lie! And if, as you say, you were having a meeting with Luke, why didn't you ask Thornwood to fetch you? Why choose to struggle home through the rain?' He released her, as if he couldn't bear to be this close, his mouth twisting with distance as he told her, 'You didn't ask for Thornwood because you didn't want him knowing where you'd spent the afternoon, he might have let something slip. So you thought it more prudent to make your own way home, regardless of what I might think when you tried to sneak in, looking like a drowned rat! Or were you counting on getting home before me?'

'Get lost!' The words were low and furious. 'You've got a sick mind.' She pushed the sodden briefcase at him. 'You'll find all my conclusions here. Luke approved them, but only because he was convinced everything he read was your idea!' she snapped bitterly, stalking away from him and stamping up the stairs.

Her anger was burned out by the time she emerged from the shower and wrapped herself in a giant blue towel. She might have expected his odious suspicions. He was paranoid where she was concerned. Nothing would convince him that she and Fenton weren't lovers. It was like a worm, eating into his soul, changing him into a man she didn't know.

Morosely, she rubbed herself dry and padded to the hanging cupboard to find something to wear. Something restrained, dignified. Because, over dinner, she was going to deliver her ultimatum. He must leave her alone, physically, allow her to use the guest-room—or to move out—until he was ready to listen to her explanation of her relationship with Robert Fenton. And then, if necessary, if he still couldn't trust her word, he could check with Luke. Luke knew Fenton had been trying to blackmail her.

Thus, bleakly and coldly decided, she reached to the back of the cupboard and pulled out a grey wool skirt, slightly flared, with its matching waistcoat. Worn with a crisp apple green shirt the outfit made her look severe and controlled. Which was precisely the effect she was aiming for.

Bolstered by her appearance—a modicum of make-up and her hair clipped back behind her ears with good old-fashioned kirby grips helped—she braced herself to deliver a mouthful of plain speaking. And at least she had her timing right, she thought relievedly as she tucked in behind Meg and the heated trolley. She would not now have to endure a pre-dinner drink with the man who so plainly found her beneath contempt, who thought lying was a way of life for her.

'Something smells good,' Cleo remarked politely. Her mind had never been further from food, but Meg always took trouble and her efforts deserved to be recognised.

The housekeeper gave her a warm, comfortable smile, 'Lamb casserole with chocolate fudge sponge to follow. You won't mind, madam, if I leave you to it?' She trundled the trolley into the drawing-room, to the small table in the alcove where Cleo and Jude often ate when they were alone to save Meg the bother of setting the huge table in the formal dining-room.

The table, Cleo noted drily, was set with two covers, candles, silver and crystal—all the right props for a romantic dinner for two. But there was no romance in this marriage, just mistrust and a whole load of agony, she mourned silently as Jude laid aside the papers he'd been concentrating on and stood up, a whisky-glass in his hand, bleak tension in his eyes.

'I was beginning to think you'd decided to go out again,' he commented bitingly.

Meg, seemingly unaware of the undercurrents that thickened the air, made the atmosphere volatile, carried on with what she'd been saying. 'Only there's a film on television we both want to watch. But I'll be down later to clear away.'

'That's fine, Meg.' Cleo had her mistress-of-the-house act honed to perfection and she smiled encouragingly as she took the hot plates and dishes from the trolley. 'Run along, Meg. I can see to this. You don't want to miss the beginning.'

She heard Jude cross the room as she ladled the herby, aromatic casserole on to plates and tried to relax muscles that had instinctively stiffened. He sat opposite her, his face stony, and as he unfolded his napkin she handed him his plate of meat and then sat in front of hers, knowing she wouldn't be able to eat a thing.

'I've skimmed through your conclusions,' he imparted coldly as he helped himself to new potatoes and courgettes. 'But I distinctly recall having asked you to consult me before putting anything in front of Luke.'

'Perhaps you did.' Those shares were the only thing he seemed interested in nowadays, she thought sourly—the only thing of hers, at least. She pushed a piece of meat around her plate, still clinging to her air of poised control because she was going to need it when she told him she would not be sharing his bed, and perhaps not even his roof, until things were resolved between them.

'You know damned well I did.' His voice was quiet, level, almost soft, and that was more nerve-racking than if he'd shouted. It was the dangerous tone he used when hauling some unfortunate Mescal Slade employee over the coals if the hapless person had had the misfortune to annoy him.

She shuddered slightly, and he must have noticed the involuntary tremor because his eyes met hers, hard and cold. He poured her a glass of burgundy, which she ignored, and she choked back hot words and found a tone to equal his.

'I don't work for you any more. You did the firing and suggested I move to Slade—if you remember.' She pushed her food around some more, just for something to do with her hands. 'I'm under no obligation to consult you at this stage. I prefer to handle this my own way.'

'The idea was,' he laid his cutlery aside, eyeing her frigidly, 'that we should work together to get the company back on its feet. Or had you forgotten?'

The look he gave her made her want to run away and hide, but she resisted the cowardly impulse and draped one arm over the back of her chair, achieving a casual elegance she was proud of, and told him dismissively, 'It was your idea, not mine. In any case, I don't quite see how it could be managed without a certain degree of accord—something which our relationship distinctly lacks. So I do this alone, or not at all. And talking of togetherness——' she ousted yet another cowardly surge of desire to remove herself from the room and studiedly re-applied herself to her cooling food, even managing to get a tiny onion as far as her mouth '—I'm going to have to insist that we sleep separately from now on. I want nothing more to do with you physically until——'

'Why not?' he cut in smoothly, giving her no time to finish what she had intended to say. 'When you enjoy it so much. We both know I only have to touch you to turn you on.'

And that left her floundering, her cheeks flaming. It was precisely because he could so easily make her want him, need him, abandon her scruples, that she had to sleep alone! She could endure the feeling of degradation no longer!

'Or is it because you are seeing Fenton again, getting all the satisfaction you can handle?' he added silkily, his eyes slitted and dangerous.

Blinking back the pain of incipient tears, fighting the racking ache in her chest, she pushed herself out of her chair. She didn't have to take this! She wouldn't take it!

Her mouth set in a furious line as all pretence of control deserted her, and she ground out, 'I want a divorce.'

It was pointless to go on trying, to even pretend to hope that things could come right for them again. As soon as she'd realised he would never listen to what she had to say in her own defence she should have known it was all over. So why put herself through this agony, the agony of loving a man who only wanted to punish her, and go on punishing her—for a crime she hadn't even committed?

'I've been waiting for this.' She could almost see the violent emotion that emanated from him, and his eyes were narrowed, taking in the flush of rage that burned along her cheekbones, the glitter of angry tears in wide grey eyes. 'I've wondered when you'd get around to asking.'

At his icy words the rage left her, just like that, and she clutched at the back of her chair. Did he mean he'd been waiting for the suggestion to come from her because he wanted out of a marriage that had become intolerable? And had she unknowingly hoped, against all common sense, that he would throw every objection in the book at her, say that, despite everything he still wanted her in his life, that he needed her?

And then he did say that much, but the same words can mean different things, and her face turned paper-white as he drawled, 'Divorce you so that you can marry Fenton, with the so-called Slade Millions safely in your control? No way.' He thrust his chair back savagely, his height, his breadth of shoulder diminishing her. And his face was austere, tight-fleshed, but a derisory dent appeared at one side of his hard mouth as he told her, 'You used me to gain control of your inheritance, the money you needed to lavish on your lover in order to keep him. But it stops there. Right there. There's no way I'm going to hand you your freedom on a plate. You're my wife and that's something you're going to have to learn to live with. And I mean live with. While you're my wife you'll share my roof-space, share my bed.'

It was the most demeaning thing he could have said to her, and she didn't know whether she loved him or hated him now. Both, she supposed, the one being almost indistinguishable from the other. And misery and shame goaded her on.

'There's nothing to stop me walking out on you and going to him,' she flashed recklessly, stung by his hateful words, saying anything at all she could think of that might hurt him as much as he had repeatedly hurt her. And strangely, she felt back in control again, almost coldly so, with only a residue of fury left to inject a very slight tremor into her voice as she curled her mouth down in a sneer. 'According to the way you view me, I'm not the type of woman to balk at walking out on my husband and going to live with my lover.'

There was just a moment of complete silence, very still, heavy, just one moment when she felt she had the upper hand, though she knew she didn't want it. And then he warned, his voice like ice, 'Do that, and I will drag you back, kicking and screaming. And that's a promise. Wherever you go, I'll find you, and make you pay, and go on paying.'

CHAPTER TEN

CLEO spent the next ten days at Slade House. She had left a terse note for Jude, telling him where she was going, and had explained to a sympathetic Meg that she needed to spend time with her uncle, who was a sick man.

She could have gone to her former home, but she'd heard that a firm offer had been made for the property in Bow. Besides, Jude would have had no hesitation in dragging her back, but even he would think twice about the wisdom of dragging her from her uncle's home.

Most of her days were spent in the office in Eastcheap with Luke and others of the board, and she managed to ignore his surly attitude, taking what comfort she could from the knowledge that her plans for Slade Securities looked like working—with no help from Jude. And Grace had confided that her husband seemed much better, more relaxed, now Cleo had joined the company. And that information had to be welcome, not only because of the improvement in John Slade's health but because it meant, in some measure, that Grace was almost ready to accept her at last. Her remark must have cost her something, since it hardly flattered her beloved son!

But today she had opted to stay at Slade House, seeking John's approval for her plans for careful expansion in some areas now that her cutbacks had gone through. She couldn't trust Luke's judgement, and she was damned if she'd ask Jude for his opinion. This was something she had to steer along herself.

Gratifyingly, although she'd had no doubts herself, her uncle had approved her projections.

'I don't think you'll ever really know how pleased I am to have you pulling for the old firm,' he said, closing the last file. 'It made no sense for you to join Mescal Slade.'

Since Cleo could hardly tell her uncle that the prospect of working with his son had given her the mental shudders, she said nothing. She was steering Slade Securities on a steadier track and that was something she was proud of. And, as it was all she had, she clung on to it tightly.

There would have to be a board meeting, of course, before some of her schemes got off the ground, and Jude would naturally be invited along in his capacity of a major shareholder, and maybe he would be offered a seat on the board... She didn't know yet.

And there was another thing he would have to be consulted about... Two days ago she had learned she was pregnant. She didn't know how or when she would break the news...

'Shall we indulge in a glass of Manzanilla? I think we deserve a celebration!' John Slade was on his feet and his old eyes were actually twinkling, and Cleo dragged her mind back to him.

'I'd like that.'

'And how much longer can I look forward to having you here?' he asked as he put the heavy, fluted Georgian glass in her hands.

'I'm not sure.' Cleo sipped the pale golden liquid, not knowing what to say. She had been here ten days already and would have to move on soon. But where? Back to Jude?

She felt safe here, protected. Her uncle had made no secret of his delight when she'd arrived, making the excuse that in her early days as Luke's working partner it would be more sensible for her to base herself here, driving into town each day with Luke and, if necessary, working on with him until the small hours.

But already there was a look in Grace's eyes that hinted at an astonishment that a relatively new bride would willingly separate herself from her devoted husband for this length of time. And only this morning, coming across Luke as he'd finished his solitary breakfast, he had sneered, 'Moved in for the duration, have you? So what happened? Did Jude find out about your involvement with Fenton and throw you out? I wouldn't blame him—I wouldn't want a wife who'd learned all there was to learn from a creep like Robert Fenton.'

Yes, she'd been marking time, but soon, very soon, she would have to decide what to do, where to go. The thought of resuming her marriage, as it had been, made her go cold, but the thought of ending the marriage made her feel worse.

And yet, on the positive side, when Jude learned she was expecting his child—and a child had been his main reason for marrying at all, with the shares thrown in as a welcome bonus—then surely he would be at last willing to listen to her side of the story, if only for the sake of the child to come? And, having listened, he would have to admit he'd been wrong...

'Selfishly, I hope you'll stay another few days,' John Slade was saying. 'But I'll understand if you're impatient to get back to Jude. So why don't you ask him to join you here, just for the weekend?'

Blinking, dragged from her reverie, Cleo managed a non-committal smile. She had come here to gain a brief respite from Jude and the problems of their marriage, so she wasn't about to ask him to join her! She needed time to think, and she couldn't think straight when he was around. But so far the thinking hadn't been done, the very idea of him had her emotions churning, too confused to be sorted out.

'I'll see if lunch is ready,' she told her uncle. The conversation was following paths she didn't want to tread. 'You just relax and finish your drink.'

Leaning against the smooth, cool wood of the study door, she forced herself to take deep, calming breaths. Jude would have to put aside his pride and listen to what she had to say—especially after she'd told him about the baby. It would take time for him to come to terms with the news that he was about to become a parent; she was only just beginning to come to terms with it herself. But then, perhaps, they could start again, try to rebuild the relationship his distrust had shattered.

Maybe she would phone him this evening, suggest they meet somewhere, on neutral ground to discuss their future...

Thus decided, she began to walk along the corridor towards the main hall at the front of the house; the luxurious silence was broken by the sound of her aunt's voice, pitched higher than was normal. 'Jude—what a lovely surprise! You're just in time for lunch. We'll go and find Cleo, shall we? She'll be delighted!'

So he had come to fetch her back! There could be no other explanation for his unexpected arrival, and Cleo's insides felt like jelly and her heart was beating too fast. He had her metaphorically cornered, there was no place to hide. Rather than have them come across her skulking in the shadows, she walked rapidly forward and tried to look pleased and surprised when she turned into the wide main hall, because her aunt's eyes would be on her and that lady was no fool—she would be quick to pick up bad vibes.

'Jude! I didn't expect you—how nice!'

Her pasted smile wobbled at that last lie, and disappeared totally when he answered suavely, 'Yes, isn't it? Nice for both of us.' His smile was warm enough but the azure eyes, set between thickly fringing black lashes, were quite cold. He turned to Grace, his poise, his outward charm, masking a taut purposefulness that only Cleo could detect, and she shuddered uncontrollably as he apologised, 'Lunch would have been delightful, Grace. But I promised myself I'd take Cleo for a break—she's been working much too hard lately. So I've planned a second mini-honeymoon.' A smooth movement gathered Cleo into the crook of his arm and she stood rigidly still, knowing this was a deadly game. She was sickeningly afraid of the outcome. 'I would have come for you sooner,' he was telling her silkily, 'but I got bogged down in endless meetings.' He made it sound like an apology, but the pressure of his hard fingers as they bit into the soft flesh just below her ribs told a different story. 'So, if you'll forgive the rush, Grace, I suggest Cleo throws her things together. We've quite a drive ahead of us.'

'But of course!' Grace's eyes, as they flickered between the two of them, were alight with approval. She had really taken to her new nephew-in-law, Cleo thought dully. Grace thought he was the best thing to happen to the Slade family in a long time.

Although she knew she was being manipulated, that a second honeymoon, a break for his hard-working, adored wife, was the last thing Jude had in mind, she tried to smile, to look happy. Her fight with her husband was a private thing, dark, demanding and devious. She would do anything to prevent it becoming public knowledge.

She had little choice but to obey Jude's smoothly worded yet heavily loaded instructions, she thought as a few minutes later she was bundling the things she'd brought with her into her suitcase. To have put up any objection, no matter how slight, would have been useless in the face of his sugar-coated determination. Besides, it would have alerted her uncle and aunt to the dark nuances of their private life. And that she did not want.

Sitting beside him in the Jaguar XJS he used when he drove himself, Cleo was lost for words. She picked a few openers over in her mind and abandoned them with a bleak compression of her lips. Whatever she said would only result in a row. He had fetched her from Slade House because she was his property, a fact he had been known to point out to her before!

Before too long she was going to have to tell him about the baby, and she didn't want to impart such wonderful information on the heels of yet another row. And she would have to choose her moment carefully because she hoped—oh, how she hoped!—that together they could talk things over and try to make the future come right.

He didn't have to love her, she confessed to herself with a deep-seated disgust at her own humility, but if he could only revert to feeling about her the way he had, with respect and liking, then it would be something she could work on.

She closed her eyes, the bright sunlight of late spring mocking her depression. But she willed herself to relax, to find some of the strength she would need when Jude at last thought fit to break his scathing silence. And eventually she sank into an uncomfortable dozing state, the tension that stretched edgily between them unabated as mind images, rather than dreams, tormented her jumpy brain. They were all of Jude—of the way he had been and the way he was—and she snapped back into full consciousness and became immediately aware that they were passing through deep countryside, unfamiliar to her.

'Been enjoying the sleep of the just?' His words were edged with sarcasm, telling her that he had known precisely when she had opened her eyes. 'Have I ever told you that you look innocent, like a child, when you sleep?'

She ignored that opening gambit. It was an invitation to yet another attack and she wasn't going to oblige him. Instead, finding a level tone, she asked, 'Are you making a detour for some reason? We should be back in town by now, surely?'

'When you chose to run away you left me with no option but to bring you back,' he replied obliquely, his profile ungiving.

'I did not run away!' she snapped, unable to prevent the hot words coming. Their future was precariously balanced, not to mention their child's, and this infighting wouldn't achieve anything useful, she was well aware of that. But she didn't see why she should always be put in the wrong. 'You knew where I was, and why,' she qualified stonily.

'I knew you'd run out on me. You could have worked with Luke just as easily from home,' he stated unequivocally. And, morosely, she supposed he was right. She had been running away from a situation that was intolerable.

And as if he'd read her thoughts, he told her levelly, 'Things can't go on as they are,' and she wondered, with a wrench of pain, if he'd decided to go for a divorce, after all. He could be extracting no pleasure from the bitter thing their marriage had become. Even his revenge, his need to humiliate her, had to lose its savour eventually.

'So what are you going to do about it?' She heard herself sounding surly, though that hadn't been her intention, and averted her head to stare out of the window, appalled by the ready sting of tears in her eyes, determined he shouldn't see them, because that would be the final humiliation.

'Start talking it out,' he informed her coldly. 'It's more than time.' He changed gear smoothly and gentled the softly growling vehicle through tight bends which had clusters of stone cottages on either side, and the tiny flicker of hope his words had brought to life was doused by the acid of past experience.

'Do you mean you'll actually let me get a word in among those accusations you're so good at?'

She bit the words out snappily then, for some reason, began to tremble as he told her, 'That's why I decided to borrow Fiona's cottage for a day or two. We can have complete privacy—and I've a feeling we're going to need it. I've a few things to say to you, and no doubt you'll have more than a few to say back,' he added drily, halting at a leafy intersection and peering at an ancient finger post.

'It's quite a time since I visted,' he imparted with the coolness of a stranger, and she stared at him, hardly able to believe that he had actually gone to such lengths in order to talk things out. And he was saying, 'Fiona's in Paris at the moment. Part business, part pleasure, so we shall have the place entirely to ourselves.'

A few hours ago that thought would have appalled her. She had gone to Slade House to escape the torment of living with him. But now, he had said he wanted to talk things out, would allow her to have her say, and that was progress. A tingle of real hope rippled through her, and she was looking through rose-tinted glasses when they drew up in front of a squat stone cottage bordering the narrow lane, and Jude introduced, 'Fiona's hideaway. Small but secluded.'

'It's perfect!' It was tiny, like a child's drawing, a straight, peony-bordered path leading from the wicket to the centrally set front door. The rest of the garden was given over to vegetables in tidy rows.

Cleo couldn't imagine Jude's elegant sister barrowing manure, forking and hoeing, and Jude, following her thoughts in the almost uncanny way he had, said, 'An old boy from the village has the use of the garden in return for keeping an eye on the place. It works well. He gets all the fresh fruit and vegetables he needs, and she feels the place is safer from the attention of vandals if it looks as if someone with a spade is about to come out of the garden shed.'

Smiling, he handed her a key. It was the first real smile she'd had from him since he'd walked in and found her with Fenton. It was a smile she could have lost herself in and her heart picked up speed, pattering rapidly, making her feel like a love-sick fool.

'Let yourself in,' he said. 'Look around while I pull the car up into the orchard. It's the only gateway wide enough.'

She walked slowly along the path, enjoying the warmth of the late afternoon sun, the fresh country smells. Life was beginning to wear a happier face. And as for their marriage, well, maybe the symptoms were grim, but the prognosis was good. It would have to be. She would make it so!

The key turned easily in the lock and Cleo stepped straight into a parlour that might have been modelled on an illustration in a Beatrix Potter book. Red and white checked curtains decked the tiny windows, rag rugs were scattered about the floor and squashy, slightly shabby flower-patterned armchairs surrounded an open fireplace, while four ladder-backed chairs were placed around a pine table which sported a vase of dried teasles.

A dresser and a rocking chair completed the décor, and Cleo gave Fiona full marks for not turning the interior of her country cottage into something artfully twee.

The whole cottage, she discovered, was basic, functional, and just right. True, there was only one bedroom, the second having been converted to a bathroom at some time. But if everything went as she prayed it would, she need have no reservations about sharing that big brass bed with Jude.

Going swiftly back down the twisting stairs, she told herself to take it easy. Pointless to hope for too much. Every time she'd tried to talk to him in the past, to put her point of view, they'd ended up further apart than before. But despite her warnings to herself she couldn't help hoping...

She found him in the kitchen; her suitcase was on the floor with a battered canvas tote bag beside it, and there was a carton of groceries on the table.

'I'll get out of this stifling gear.' He indicated his formal grey business suit and picked up her suitcase, the tote bag which must contain his things. 'Like the place?' he asked, turning in the low doorway, and there was a softness in his eyes that warmed her heart. She couldn't help smiling, her pleasure showing through the cool façade.

'I love it!' She would have said the same if he had brought her to stay in a hen house, because she just knew everything was going to be fine.

'Good.' He made a movement as if to go on his way, but something seemed to hold him and she saw, just for a second, a look of puzzlement deep in his eyes. And then it was gone, and it might never have been because the azure depths were as they so often were—slightly on the cold side of bland—before he finally turned away.

As she heard his feet on the stairs she turned to the box he'd left on the table. Unpacking it would give her something to do, calm her. She felt slightly sick, every sense highly tuned because, one way or another, the next day or so would set the pattern for the rest of her life.

The box was crammed with enough food to last them for days and she moved about the kitchen quickly, stowing a fresh chicken, butter and bacon in the fridge, leaving the steak out because they could have that tonight. She was crouching, pushing the cartons of milk into the already full fridge, when he said, from behind her, 'I'm going to split logs. I'll light a fire, the evenings get chilly.'

She turned, looking up at him over her shoulder, and her heart flopped over. He had changed and he looked, as ever, superb. Faded denim jeans clipped long legs and lean hips, and his dark checked shirt had long sleeves, pulled up to the elbows, revealing hard, sinewy forearms liberally sprinkled with dark hair. And she only had to look at him to know she would always love him, no matter what happened.

'Perhaps you could make a start on a meal,' he suggested. 'We both missed lunch.' He was leaning against the table, half sitting, seemingly relaxed, and she was about to tell him, fine, she'd do just that because suddenly she was hungry, too, when the words died in her throat as he said softly, 'You look washed out, despite the sleep you had coming down here. Been pining over the news?'

'What news?' She was reluctant to tell him that her sleepless nights had been caused by her misery over him, and she stood up slowly, closing the fridge door with a nudge of her knee, repeating, 'What news? What are you talking about?'

'Fenton's engagement to Livia Haine, the millionaire brewer's daughter.' His mouth dented derisively. 'You can take it from me, they deserve each other. She's a first-class bitch.'

'I didn't know.' Her heart began to thump, sounding thunderous in her own ears. Fenton engaged? It was the best news she'd heard in years! If he was set to marry money, which had always been his ambition, then he would keep his act clean until he'd secured the lady with a plain gold ring. He must have been working on it, and that would be why she'd heard no more from him. Unsavoury details, involving his debts, wouldn't be what he'd want to see splashed around in some sordid gossip column. She was safe from Robert Fenton at last!

Carefully keeping her face straight, she pushed a strand of silvery hair back from her face with the back of her hand. 'I hadn't heard.'

'No?' Jude said. 'Didn't he at least warn you to expect that sickening photograph in the papers yesterday, alongside the announcement of their engagement? Apparently,' he added drily, 'it was a whirlwind romance.'

She didn't care what kind of romance it had been, and if Jude was right and the lady in question was a bitch then she wasn't about to waste her sympathy on her behalf. And she was about to say just that when he forestalled her again, levering himself away from the table, his face expressionless.

'I thought, with Fenton out of your reach, we could talk things through, lay out the guidelines for our future, our marriage. Because, believe me, he won't want to continue with your relationship if he's got his hooks into another heiress—one who's free to marry him.'

And with that he strode from the room, leaving her gaping. He must have decided to borrow the cottage, to fetch her away from Slade House, when he'd learned of

Fenton's engagement. What he'd said hadn't been flattering, but at least he was willing to talk things through, try to make their marriage work. And he would listen to what she had to tell him, and they could begin again.

She could understand his initial revulsion when he'd walked in on what must have appeared to be a torrid love scene between herself and Fenton. But she hadn't been able to understand why he had refused to hear her defence. After all, it wasn't as if his emotions were involved...

Her hands shook a little as she washed the salad they would eat with the steak, her insides wriggling around with what she recognised as nervous excitement. If theirs had been a normal marriage she wouldn't be feeling this way. She would have been desperately hurt by his total lack of trust, her love for him terminally ill by now because the type of mistrust he harboured couldn't co-exist with love.

But he had never loved her, never pretended to. The love was all on her side, and she'd known she would have to be the one to make their marriage a workable thing. And now, at last, she was going to be able to work on it again.

Reaching the steaks out of the fridge, she paused, undecided. She could still hear the regular sound of the axe and it looked as though Jude was all set to split enough wood to last through a month of chilly evenings. That being so, the meal could wait for the time it would take her to freshen herself up.

Her mind made up, she was already at the door to the stairway when Jude came in from outside, a pile of logs in his arms, and she halted, uncertain of what to do.

'Would you like me to put the steaks on now, or have I got time to change first?' she asked, her colour rising as his blue eyes lazily swept her slender jeans and shirt-clad figure. There was a hint, just a hint, of the old warmth in the look he gave her and her heart flipped over with love for him. Everything was going to be all right; she had never been more certain of anything.

'You look good to me as you are.' His gaze lingered on her rumpled hair. 'But if it makes you feel better, go ahead and change. But don't take all night about it, we've a lot of talking to do.'

And that was vastly reassuring. He had said he'd listen to what she had to say, and at last he was talking to her as an equal, his voice softer than she'd heard it for weeks—not bitingly bitter, as it had been, coming out as if he hated her, felt her to be beneath contempt.

She shot him a grateful look, unable to stop herself, to disguise her love. Not that she wanted to, not now, not ever again.

After showering quickly in the tiny bathroom, she rummaged through her suitcase, making a mental note to unpack before going to bed. But, for now, she picked out fresh oyster satin lace underwear and a fine wool sweater dress. Although the day had been bright and warm, the evening, as Jude had prophesied, was turning chilly. The very thought of him made slow colour burn over her skin as she wriggled into the soft wool dress.

The shade of muted peacock green suited her and the garment fitted her perfectly, skimming her slender body without a wrinkle or ruck. The deep V of the neckline created a shadowy cleft between her breasts and, unconsciously, she twisted in front of the mirror, running the palms of her hands over the flat plane of her stomach.

There was no sign of any swelling, but then there wouldn't be yet, and she bit softly on her full lower lip, filled with an unfathomable love for the tiny life she carried, for the man who had fathered her child. Then she turned away quickly, heading out of the room, filled with an emotion so intense it threatened to explode inside her unless something was done about it, and quickly!

She would tell Jude about the baby over dinner—if not before! She couldn't wait a moment longer to share this wonderful secret with him. Explanations about Robert Fenton could wait until later—she had to tell Jude about the baby they had made, because nothing could be as important as that.

Her feet were light as she ran downstairs to the kitchen, her heart even lighter, but her face fell as she realised Jude already had their meal in the final stages of preparation. She felt cheated, she had wanted to make the meal—a labour of love! Then, smiling at her own silliness, she advanced into the room, sniffing at the delicious aroma of grilling steak and Jude looked up from the crusty granary loaf he'd been slicing and caught her smile, returning it, but guardedly.

'You look good enough to eat,' His eyes swept appraisingly over her lovingly encased body. 'But I couldn't wait. I missed breakfast, too.'

'Can I help?' Suddenly, Cleo was unaccountably shy and was almost relieved when he shook his head, a lock of dark, rumpled hair falling over one eye, giving him a rakish look that set her heart tipping wildly.

'Nope. It's all done. We'll eat in the living-room—go through and pour the wine. There's not room for both of us in here—but you can take the bread with you.'

If the words were clipped in a dismissive tone, she didn't really mind. In his mind nothing had changed and there was still a lot of talking to do, his so-called guidelines for their future to be mapped out. He didn't know, as she did, that there was nothing to worry about and never had been.

He had spread a red-checked cloth that matched the curtains over the table, and the glow from the crackling log fire and the single side-lamp darkened the sky outside the windows to amethyst. She put the bread on the table, near the salad in its shallow glass bowl, smiling as she noticed the careful place settings, the wineglasses, the unlit candle in a porcelain holder shaped like a rose.

He had gone to a lot of trouble and, still smiling softly, she lit the candle and poured the wine, taking her own glass to stand near a window, looking out. The first stars were beginning to blink in the darkening sky, the land shadows merging into a dusky pall, and she knew that before the sun rose again she and Jude would be embarking on a marriage that would certainly have real meaning for her and, hopefully, for him, too.

'Come and get it.' His voice, behind her, startled her into turning quickly and she almost spilled her wine. In the softly diffused glow of light that illuminated the little room his features looked more mellow, his mouth gentler. But his eyes were unreadable, deeply shadowed, and she didn't know what he was thinking.

The steaks were perfectly cooked, but Cleo's appetite had deserted her and she toyed with her food as she watched him hungrily eat his. She was going to have to tell him about the baby, she could contain the secret no longer. And his pleasure would be her pleasure. No, more than pleasure—a deep and ecstatic happiness.

He had talked of children before. Getting children had been the only reason he had married at all. But she had seen their children as abstract things, mere shadowy ideas. But now—this was different. Jude's child was within her, real, living, already loved, and as alive to her as her own flesh, her blood.

And she had to share this miracle with him. Now.

'Jude,' she blurted impulsively, nervous excitement making her voice thin, 'we're going to have a baby. I'm pregnant.'

She hadn't known quite what his reaction would be, but she hadn't expected the blank, shuttered expression that met her as he raised his eyes and looked at her levelly, full in the face, across the table. Nor did she understand the brief flash of pain she saw in his eyes before he laid aside his cutlery and remarked distantly, 'Congratulations. But excuse me if I don't share your dewy-eyed enthusiasm. How can I be sure it's mine, and not Fenton's?'

And something died inside her at that moment. It was hope. All hope was dead. It had struggled gallantly against all the odds and now, with those few words, it had finally expired. There was a bitter taste in her mouth, a tight pain around her heart. This was the end.

'Go to hell,' she said flatly, an indescribable pain pulling her to pieces, and he looked at her once, before thrusting his chair back and standing up, his mouth twisted downwards before he turned away.

'I've just been there.'

CHAPTER ELEVEN

JUDE slid the car to a halt outside the house in Belgravia, his features set in the tight mask he'd worn since she'd told him about the baby.

'I'll drop you off here while I garage the car.' It was the first thing he'd said during the drive home, and his words registered heavily on a mind that was still in shock.

'And Cleo——' this as her numb fingers were fumbling to release her safety belt '—have Meg move my things into the guest-room.'

A logical request, since their marriage was dead, she thought drearily, but bitterness still lived on and it surfaced in her tone as, staring straight ahead, she said tartly, 'I thought we were going to talk things out. That was the point of going to the cottage, wasn't it? I thought I was going to be allowed to put my point of view, for once.'

'Everything changed when you told me you were pregnant.' From the corner of her eye she saw his hands tighten on the steering wheel, making the knuckles white, and she thought she could detect a thread of emotion in his voice. But his tone was as before, flat, when he added, 'With Fenton off the scene, about to be married, I'd thought we might pick up the pieces, make something— no matter how superficial—of our marriage. Every time I look at your child I shall wonder if it's mine, or Fenton's, and not even I could live with that.'

'Fenton and I were never lovers!' The words came quickly, spilling out; they just had to be said, even though she knew she and Jude were finished.

He said wearily, 'Don't lie, Cleo. There's no point,' and she felt tired beyond belief, utterly drained.

Automatically, she moved out of the car and into the house, her feet somehow carrying her to the roomy kitchen where Thornwood was cleaning silver and Meg was putting vegetables through the blender for soup.

'Oh, madam! We didn't expect you home today!' Meg put a hand to her plump bosom. 'Walking in like a ghost!' And then, her startled reaction receding, her eyes narrowed in concern. 'Are you all right, madam? You're very pale.'

'I'm fine.' Cleo's smile was automatic, too. She felt numb. 'I thought I ought to let you know we're back.'

She was talking as though she and Jude were still an entity. But it wasn't the case. They had never been further apart. Even during the time when he'd looked at her with contempt, yet possessed her body with nightly, passionate savagery, there had been the unmistakable bonding of deep, racking emotion. Now there was nothing. Nothing at all.

'No, I won't have coffee, thanks,' she replied to Thornwood's offer. 'But Mr Mescal might like a tray.'

She left the room as silently as she had entered it, feeling like the wraith Meg had likened her to. The Thornwoods had been married a long time. They had grown together. Cleo couldn't imagine one without the other. Would they be able to understand the tragedy that her brief marriage to Jude had become? Probably not. For them, love and marriage would only be seen as a comfortable, comforting, easy thing.

She wouldn't ask Meg to move Jude's things, of course. That was something she had to do herself. An exorcism, perhaps. And it was what she had wanted, she reminded herself as she took formal suits and casual wear in methodical armloads from his half of the enormous hanging cupboard. She had tried to tell him she wanted to sleep alone, at least until he was willing to give her a hearing. But then, of course, there had still been the hope that having listened to her, realised his suspicions had been entirely without foundation—then, and only then, would they have been able to try to rebuild their relationship.

Now, of course, there was no hope left, and the action of clearing his things out was so completely final. It was the end, finis, nothing more to be said. The thought made her want to cry, but she didn't have the energy. The empty, defeated feeling had grown, depleting her mental resources, ever since he'd cleared the uneaten food from the table last night and had told her she might as well go and re-pack as they'd be leaving first thing in the morning.

Still shattered by what he had said about the questionable paternity of the child she was carrying, she had dragged herself upstairs, staring at her reflection and thinking how silly she looked in the pretty, clinging dress, her face a white mask punctuated by the deep dark holes of her eyes. She hadn't unpacked, so there had been nothing to do but curl up on the bed, pulling the soft eiderdown over her cold body, saying goodbye to her marriage.

Later, she had heard him leave the cottage and she'd lain awake all night, her eyes burning and dry as she'd stared into the darkness. At dawn, he had come back and she'd gone downstairs, still in the dress she'd slept in, dragging her suitcase. He had given her one hard look from empty eyes, the strain lines around his mouth making him look older. He must have been walking all night, judging by the way he looked, and immediate concern for him came to life in the emptiness of her heart, and she'd said quickly, 'Jude—sit down, let me make you some breakfast—and let's try, for pity's sake, to talk this thing out. Things are nothing like you believe them to be——'

'Forget it.' He was walking away from her. 'I don't want breakfast, and there's nothing to be said that would make any difference to the way things are.'

Ever since that he had treated her as though she didn't exist. She probably didn't, not to him, she thought as she slid the last of his shirts into the top drawer of the chest in the guest-room.

He had never pretended to love her, and as far as he was concerned he had made a bad error of judgement when he'd decided a marriage between them could work. And now he was cutting his losses, cutting her out of his life. The process, she knew, had only just begun.

'Is that the lot?' He had come into the room quietly. 'I'd have given you a hand if you'd said you weren't asking Meg to do it.' He didn't look as tired as he had done, although he was still pale beneath his tan. Meg's coffee must have helped.

Cleo hunched one shoulder, not knowing what to say. What could one say in such a situation? She wouldn't go down on her knees and beg him to listen to her. She had her pride, if nothing else.

He moved further into the room, unbuttoning his shirt, and she edged back towards the door. 'I'm going to shower and change,' he told her. He looked at her as he spoke but his eyes were empty. The light had gone out of them. 'I won't be back for dinner, so don't wait up. Let Meg know, would you?' he said dismissively, and Cleo slipped out of the door and went to her room. Tomorrow, after she'd slept, she would think of what was best to do; emulate her husband and try to cut her losses, or try to go on.

* * *

But no amount of sleep or concentrated hard work helped her to reach a decision over her future. Her days fell into a pattern she hadn't the will to break. Always, after a solitary breakfast, Thornwood, drove her to Eastcheap and collected her at six. An evening working, her papers spread out on the table in the drawing-room, followed a lonely dinner which she forced herself to eat for the sake of her child. Sometimes Jude joined her for the meal and then shut himself away in his study for the rest of the evening, but more often than not he stayed away. He didn't say where he went, or what he was doing, and Cleo didn't ask. She didn't think she cared.

There was no communication between them now, not even anger, and one day soon Cleo was going to have to answer the questions she could see building up behind Meg's eyes. The housekeeper was fond of them both, particularly of Jude, and even if she hadn't sensed the frigid atmpsphere—and she would have to be blind and deaf not to—she was well aware that they used separate bedrooms, that Jude left the house before eight each morning and was rarely back before midnight.

So sooner or later the questions would come, Meg wouldn't be able to help herself. And what could she answer? Cleo wondered tiredly. She could hardly tell Meg the truth, tell her that Jude had seen her sprawled out on the floor, semi-naked, with Robert Fenton, that he believed the child she carried was Fenton's!

It was the thought of the child that finally woke senses that had been entombed in a dull, unfeeling limbo. She had hoped to make her marriage a good thing, to teach him, eventually, to love her as she had loved him. But that hope had died and she'd be a fool if she ever thought of trying to bring it to life. And there was her unborn child to consider. No child could be expected to thrive in a house where its parents rarely met, hardly exchanged two words from one week to the next!

There would have to be a separation, or a divorce. Cleo didn't care which. And if Jude wouldn't agree then she would just have to take matters into her own hands. Move out, and soon.

Thus decided, she settled herself to wait for him. He had, apparently, told Meg he wouldn't be in for dinner, and as far as Cleo knew he hadn't yet spent the entire night away from home. But when the clock struck two in the morning she began to think there was a first time for everything, and it was then she heard the sound of the hall door closing, his footsteps, dragging, as if he were bone weary—or drunk.

Twenty-four hours ago she would have been able to face him with a dreary kind of equanimity. But her emergence from the limbo she had inhabited meant that her emotions were alive and kicking again, torturing her. All through the long waiting hours he had prowled through her mind. A silent, mistrustful, austere image. And, she had to face it, a much-loved image. Despite everything, her love for him survived. He couldn't murder that.

Now, her legs shook weakly as she went to intercept him in the hall, and a hand went up to push tiredly at her hair as she told him, 'I must talk to you.'

'Now?' The hall was dimly lit at this hour, but she could see the lines of strain around his eyes, his mouth, the shadow of stubble that darkened his tautly fleshed jaw.

'I'm afraid so. It won't wait.' She turned back into the drawing-room, her heart beating heavily. She half expected him to ignore her request, to carry on upstairs. He looked exhausted enough to fall into bed and sleep for twenty-four hours.

But he wasn't far behind her and she turned, watching him as he hooked a thumb under his tie, loosening it. And as he slopped brandy into a glass she wondered, for the first time, how he spent the evenings he stayed away from home, where he spent them, and with whom.

She wished she hadn't. Her mind conjured images she didn't want to begin to consider. And the surge of jealousy was painful, frightening.

'Well?' The question was put without any real interest, and that hurt. It was as if she were of no importance at all, something not to be considered, unless absolutely necessary.

She saw him empty his glass in one long swallow and snapped shrewishly, 'Do you need to drink like a fish?'

One dark eyebrow came up at that, but only slightly, as if her presence had registered, just a little, but was of no consequence. He turned to refill his glass, his voice cool. 'Need? Do you begin to know what I need?'

'No!' The response was pushed out of her on a gasp. 'I don't know. Not any more! But I do know this——' She dragged in a deep, ragged breath, getting hold of herself again. She couldn't get through to him on any emotional level, not any more. And, having accepted that, the only sane thing to do was to keep cool, not allow him to know how her heart was beginning the painful process of breaking up again. If she could keep her dignity, and her pride, it would at least be something. 'I know we can't go on like this,' she went on, her voice flat. 'The sort of marriage we have doesn't make any sense. The house is full of silence; you rarely speak. You're rarely at home—and your absences are unexplained. It's no atmosphere to bring up a child in.'

She sat down, too weary to stand now, her eyes pools of fatigue in the pale oval of her face, and Jude said slowly, 'Of course. The child.' His eyes drifted over her as if to find evidence of the new life. 'We mustn't forget the child.' He went to stand in front of the empty fireplace and the dry bitterness in his voice made her throat tighten. 'I am willing to accept the child, give it my name—regardless of whether it is mine or Fenton's. But in exchange, I would prefer it if you didn't instigate divorce proceedings in the near future. We can review the situation in a few years' time.'

Cleo became very still, If she moved now, or tried to speak, she knew she would go to pieces. That he wanted her to remain, legally, as his wife for a few more years meant only that he would prefer to keep up appearances. How she felt, trapped in this bitter travesty of a marriage, was neither here nor there. Then he said, as if he had previously given the matter a great deal of thought, 'However, for the sake of sanity, it would be best if we lived largely apart. The absence of the inevitable tension would obviously be better for the child, too. There would be speculation, naturally,' he continued in the same judicial tone. 'But it would seem feasible that we might have decided it to be in the child's best interests to be brought up in the country. If you'll leave it in my hands I'll arrange everything. As it happens,' his eyes flickered to her stony face, 'Fiona mentioned a property for sale a mile or so away from her weekend cottage. I'll look into the possibilities.'

'Do that,' she choked, shocked by the way she was feeling—as if she had just received a death sentence! And she knew that, although she couldn't live with him, she couldn't live without him.

In a moment she might cry. But she wouldn't shed tears in front of him—in front of the remote, cold-eyed stranger he had become. And she pushed herself to her feet, her legs distinctly unsteady as they carried her to the door. The expanse of carpeting had never seemed so wide, the privacy of her room so far away. But he was at the door before her, holding it open, telling her, 'I'll get something settled as quickly as possible. I'll keep you informed, of course, and you can vet any property I find that's suitable.'

Pausing, the words he was saying sounding more like verbal torture than a reasoned solution to a shared and bitter problem, she looked up into the hard, handsome planes of his unforgiving face and suddenly her eyes narrowed as hatred, quick and burning, filled the smoky eyes that had been huge pools of misery.

'After you're settled somewhere I will try to drop by from time to time,' he was remarking levelly as she pulled her shoulders straight, her voice like a spitting cat as she retorted,

'You won't have to waste your time. I wouldn't let you over the doorstep!'

And he could make what he liked of that, she thought as she swept past him, her head high, two spots of hectic colour blazing along her cheekbones.

As far as she was concerned there was no way their separation would resemble anything like a civilised arrangement!

She had finished with him; no more pining, no more regrets. Nothing! And she wouldn't give him the satisfaction of knowing that her violent reaction to a fairly reasonable suggestion had been sparked by the lingering fragrance of the light but definitely exotic perfume she had detected on his clothes!

He would never know that she was blindingly jealous of the woman, whoever, who wore such a distinctive perfume for him, the woman whose arms he had left before coming home to tell his wife he was in the process of finding some suitable hole to bury her in! And no one could tell her—no one!—that he hadn't been scheming and plotting to discover the best way of being rid of her long before she had told him things couldn't go on the way they were. And no wonder he didn't want a divorce just yet—a wife in the background would be the perfect let-out for a man whose mistress became too demanding!

Her fury carried her up the stairs at a pace that might have astounded her had she been capable of thinking of it. She was not going to be put where she didn't want to go! She would not be discreetly hidden away, an unwanted wife, allowing her highly sexed, highly attractive, non-committed husband to conduct amorous affairs with the beautiful, available women who would be only too delighted to bring a little warmth and comfort to his lonely life!

'So there you are! Meg said she thought you were sunning yourself.'

Cleo opened her heavy eyelids to see Fiona walking over the immaculately tended lawn at the back of the house. The small garden was Thornwood's pride, every plant treated as though it were a precious child, and it provided a corner of peace and beauty, unexpected in the heart of the sprawling, mighty city.

'No, don't move,' Fiona commanded softly, settling herself on the sun-warmed grass as Cleo swung her long legs from the sun lounger. 'You look so comfy! And congratulations on your super news! How are you, anyway?' Long, deep blue eyes—so like Jude's—narrowed as they swept Cleo's drawn features. 'Junior giving you a bad time?'

'Ah.' The wrinkle of perplexity cleared from Cleo's brow as the penny dropped. Jude must have told his sister about the baby. She wondered drily if he'd also said he believed it to be Fenton's. Cursing the colour that flooded her face at that horrible thought she lay back, trying to look relaxed. 'A little.'

It was nothing like the truth. Jude's baby wasn't giving her a bad time, and if it ever did she wouldn't complain. Her baby was the only thing she had and already she loved it with a fierce maternalism that amazed her. The coming child meant more to her than her high-powered job, her private fortune, more than Jude. Much more. Unconsciously, her mouth formed a grim, straight line. She had cut Jude out of her life. He was devious, cruel and she was well rid of him.

'How was the Paris trip?' Cleo carefully turned the subject, but Fiona was having none of that.

'Fine,' she dismissed with a throwaway gesture of long-fingered hands. 'But I didn't break into my lazy holiday to talk about that.' She wriggled out of the short-sleeved jacket of her silvery-grey cotton skirt suit and the hot sun caressed the skin of her bare arms, turning it gold. 'Jude tells me you're working too hard. I'm glad to see you taking it easy today.'

That surprised her; she didn't think he noticed what she did, or cared. But she wasn't going to be the one to explain that the marriage was over. 'I didn't feel like going in today. Maybe I'll get something done at home this afternoon.' And that was the truth. Another day cooped up with Luke had been more than she could face this morning. Jealous fury had kept her awake most of the night and she'd surfaced at dawn, determined to do as Jude had obviously done, and cut her losses, decide for herself what to do with her life.

'He also told me you were on the look-out for a country home—somewhere to bring the baby up in,' Fiona said slowly, and Cleo asked, her mouth dry,

'When did you see him?

Had Jude confided in his sister, told her his marriage was over? They were very close...

'Last night.' Fiona plucked at the silky fabric of her scarlet sleeveless top, the heat in the sun-trap of the garden getting to her. 'He came to the cottage where I'm supposed to be treating myself to a spot of relaxation after the madhouse of the Paris fashion world. And the upshot was, I've never felt less relaxed in my life.' The blue eyes were shrewd. 'Look—I've got a lot to say to you, but I'm parched. Why don't I ask Meg if she can find us a long, cool drink?'

'I'm sorry—let me go——'

Cleo was on her feet, annoyed with herself for her lack of hospitality, but Fiona had a mind of her own and was on her feet, too, standing close as she instructed, 'I'll do it. Stay here and rest. And that's an order!'

Cleo frowned, her eyes finding her sister-in-law's, puzzled. 'The perfume you're wearing?' she asked slowly. 'Were you wearing it last night?'

'Sure.' Fiona looked as though she thought Cleo had gone slightly mad. Then she smiled disarmingly, 'I've been drenching myself in the stuff ever since I had it made up for me in Paris. Like it? There's this little place—they blend fragrances for individual customers. Cost the earth—but worth it!'

She swung away, up the short flight of stone steps that led to the terrace, disappearing into the house through the open french windows of Jude's study, and Cleo sank down on the grass, her head resting on her jean-clad knees. The relief was overwhelming, stupidly, gloriously overwhelming.

Jude hadn't been womanising last night. He had been visiting his sister, and it was her perfume that had clung to his clothes! The knowledge shouldn't have made any difference—nothing could alter the fact that their marriage was over—but it did. But it made her feel vulnerable again, consumed with pain, because the reason for her fury was gone, undermining her grim determination to cut him completely out of her life, to make her future empty of even the memory of him.

'Our luck's in!' Fiona appeared with two tall glasses, ice-cubes clinking. 'Freshly made lemon juice——' She handed Cleo a glass and sank down beside her, sipping her drink thirstily. And when the last drop was gone she put the glass aside and said seriously, 'I'm about to interfere—with no apologies whatsoever. There's something badly wrong between you and Jude, and don't explode——' this as Cleo spluttered on her drink '—because it won't do any good. I intend to get at the truth.'

Cleo put her glass aside and stared Fiona straight in the eyes. 'Just what did Jude tell you?' Her stomach was tying itself in knots. Fiona meant well, but she was probing an open wound. No amount of interference on her part could alter a single damn thing!

'Nothing,' Fiona disclaimed. 'But he didn't need to. He arrived at the cottage around nine, looking like death, and he hung around until almost one—despite the heavy hints I dropped about needing my beauty sleep. And towards the end of our rather draggy conversation he let drop that he was looking for a country property for you to retire to—like immediately—in order to give the baby, when it comes, the space and freedom to run around in. And when I mentioned that Dene Place, not far from my cottage, was on the market he said it could well be the answer, if it was remotely suitable, as I'd be on hand most weekends to give you some company. Now I'm not a fool, Cleo,' Fiona stated the obvious, examining her fingernails with absorbed interest. 'Firstly, when he told me about the baby there was nothing coming over from him—no pride, excitement, nothing. He might as well have been telling me you'd ordered a new set of pans for the kitchen. And as for a country house, for you and baby to immure yourselves in—well, that makes no kind of sense. Even I, who scarcely know one end of a baby from the other, know it would be some time after it was born before it could go romping merrily through meadows and climbing trees and fishing in the brook.'

She spread her hands, still regarding them intently, and Cleo felt sick as Fiona went on slowly, deliberately, 'A country place would be fine for weekends and so forth—but as a permanent thing, for a pregnant lady and, later, a mum with a small round bundle under one arm, no way. So I decided that as I was unlikely to get any sense out of that dumb brother of mine I'd come and harass you. And what I see doesn't offer much comfort. So what goes on, Cleo?'

But Cleo couldn't answer; the words simply couldn't get past the painful lump in her chest. She would have given anything at that moment to be hard enough to achieve a brittle smile, to say not to worry because there was nothing to worry about. That she and Jude had decided, quite amicably, to call it a day—no hard feelings on either side. But that was something she could never do. Despite everything, her love for Jude ran too deep for that. It was still real, alive, and hurting. She had received very little affection in her life since her parents had died, and love, when she had finally experienced it, was too precious, even now, to sully with lies.

'Jude means a lot to me,' Fiona said softly, her blue eyes compassionate as they held the grey, dark-ringed ones. 'And when I first saw you two together I knew you were right for each other. I'd always known it would take a special kind of lady to snare the hard man's heart. And I was glad to know he'd found her at last.'

Those words, the very real affection in Fiona's voice, were Cleo's undoing. She had never snared Jude's heart—she'd merely captured his interest with the offer of those shares, the statement of fact when she'd told him he could always be sure she hadn't married him for his money. She'd alerted the logical brain to her possibilities as a wife at a time when he'd been considering marriage for the sake of an heir.

Unstoppable sobs shook her slender frame and Fiona's arm, coming swiftly around her shoulders, opened the floodgates. Between deep, painful sobs, the tears she thought she had cried all out, the whole dreadful, tragic story of their brief stormy marriage was told.

'You mean that louse was trying to blackmail you and that pig-headed, obstinate brother of mine refused to listen to a word you said?' Fiona pushed a slippery strand of pale hair back from Cleo's flushed face. 'You poor baby.'

There was a crusading note in Fiona's voice and Cleo's eyes clouded with panic.

'Please,' she said, her voice thick, 'promise me you won't say anything to Jude?'

'It's time someone made him listen to the truth.' Fiona's mouth firmed. 'You are both fine, beautiful, brainy people, but as far as the emotions are concerned you haven't enough gumption between you to figure your way from A to B!'

'Please!' Even to her own ears, Cleo sounded demented. But Fiona simply didn't understand! How could she, when she hadn't lived through the searing agony of it all? Somehow, though, she had to try to make her understand a little of the way it was. Desperately, she clutched at the other woman's hands.

'Don't you see——' she appealed, her eyes intense. 'Telling Jude the truth now wouldn't mean a thing. We got along fine to begin with, I grant you that, and I had begun to hope he'd learn to love me.' Her voice wobbled at that, at the hurting memory of hopes long dead, but she forced herself to go on because it was important. 'He never did love me, it was a marriage of convenience, simply that. And things started to go wrong before he could begin to develop any deep feelings for me. He began to despise me for what he thought I was. It's understandable, if you stop to think about it. He didn't love me, so he had no real reason to question the evidence of his eyes, and I suppose I had too much pride to stand there and bellow and force him to listen to what I had to say. In a peculiar kind of way I felt he had to ask me for the truth, or at least to show a willingness to listen whenever I tried to bring it up.' She shrugged wearily. 'I thought that if I was beginning to mean anything to him at all he surely must want to hear my side of things. But he didn't, of course, because all the time his dislike of me was hardening. He'd made a bad mistake in marrying me and he wanted me out of his life. And if you think about it you'll realise for him there can be no going back to the days when he thought I was a reasonable proposition as a wife, the mother of his children. So promise me, Fiona,' her grip tightened, 'promise you won't say a word. The truth might make him feel uncomfortable—bad, even—but what's the point of that? There's been too much mistrust, contempt, to make our marriage even begin to look like working again. If there'd been love on his side, too, then it might have stood a chance. But there never was. It's better for both of us to make a clean break. So please promise you'll say nothing?'

Fiona stood up, disentangling her hands, her face strained.

'If it's what you want to hear and it will put your mind at rest, then all right, my dear. I promise.'

CHAPTER TWELVE

'THE estate agents' particulars are in here.' He passed her a large envelope then fastened his seat-belt. 'You might like to glance at them on the journey.'

'Thank you,' she said stiffly, her words almost inaudible, and as the Jag turned out of the quiet, early morning London square her fingers tightened on the envelope. She knew she would make little sense of the contents, even if the particulars of the house they were going to view had been written for an idiot's consumption.

It was going to be another glorious day, the sun already warm as it streamed through the window at her side. Jude was casually dressed in lightweight stone-coloured jeans, a black body-hugging T-shirt that emphasised the whiplash power of his shoulders and chest. But there was nothing casual about his attitude; she could feel the tension in him and it was as tightly coiled as her own. Her edginess was reaching impossible proportions, every one of her senses sharply aware of every move he made, every breath he took.

Until last night she hadn't seen him since he'd told her it would be better if they lived apart. He hadn't been home. If he'd been away on a business trip she hadn't known about it and she'd had too much pride to ask. But last night he'd come to her room, tapping on the door politely, like a stranger. She'd been already in bed, sitting up staring blankly at nothing as she'd tried to bring her mind to the point of making plans for her future, where she would go, and when.

'I picked up the keys to Dene Place,' he'd told her flatly, his eyes a stranger's eyes in the gauntness of his face. 'I'll drive you down to take a look at it tomorrow. We might as well make an early start. Eight o'clock?'

And on that he had gone, closing the door quietly behind him, tangible evidence of the way he had shut her out of his life.

Three days ago she would have told him to get lost, that she could find a place on her own, didn't need his help. But since that traumatic conversation with Fiona she had done some serious thinking. It was pointless to be on the defensive, to fight. Her relationship with Jude was written out, the end of a chapter in her life. It was something she had to accept, no matter how painful, so there was no point in making things even more difficult.

As for Dene Place—well, if it was remotely suitable then she and her child might as well live there as anywhere else. At least Fiona would be around most weekends, and that was a plus. She had taken an instinctive liking to Jude's sister and she knew all there was to know about their disastrous marriage. There would never be any need to pretend with her; Fiona was on her side, and that had to count for something.

A sigh was dragged from her, right up from her toes, and although she'd been scarcely aware of it, absorbed in her thoughts, it had registered with Jude and he said roughly, 'It will soon be over, Cleo.'

Her eyes flicked to him briefly, noting the twist of his mouth, the hard bones of his profile jutting against the taut skin. Was he talking about the journey? Or the sick farce of their marriage? She didn't know and she wasn't asking, and she closed her eyes and didn't open them again until the car drew to a halt and he cut the engine.

They were parked in front of tall wrought-iron gates, set between stone posts, and Jude got out. 'I'll open the gates.' Cleo slid out of her seat, closing the car door behind her.

'I'll walk up,' she told him, passing him as he swung the gates open. The iron creaked as it moved on its rusty hinges and she didn't look at him. It hurt too much.

She would look over the house, and if she liked it she would buy it. And she'd move in as soon as remotely possible, install a computer link-up with Slade head office, go on from there. For the sake of appearances, Jude didn't want a divorce just yet and neither, particularly, did she. She would never re-marry, and as for being free—well, she'd never be free of him, she knew that, because she would always love him. Love him, hate him, there seemed little difference.

Once today was over she probably wouldn't have to see him again, or not very often. He'd continue to make himself scarce until she was settled in a place of her own. She knew he wouldn't want to spend time with her.

Dene Place was a Queen Anne house, not too large, and the gardens were a wilderness, but the fabric of the building seemed sound. The bare, dusty floorboards echoed with the hollow sound common to all empty houses as she explored, leaving him to follow if he felt he had to.

The view from the first-floor windows was benignly rural—meadows, trees, gentle hills—and she could be reasonably content here.

'What do you think?' Jude had walked up behind her and she stiffened, her eyes staring, not seeing anything now. Then she made herself turn, a slight smile pinned to her face, and he was closer than she had expected.

Her bare arm brushed against his and the shock made her stumble. He put a hand out to steady her, the action automatic, and she sucked in her breath, moving away quickly. His slightest touch still set her alight. There was nothing she could do about it.

'I like it,' she took up his question, anxious that he shouldn't guess how he still affected her physically. 'I'll buy, subject to surveyors' reports, and I'll handle the whole thing. There's no need for you to put yourself to any more trouble.' She wanted the thing settled now, and this place would be somewhere to hide, to lick her wounds.

'It's not too isolated for you?'

Her eyes fled to his, hard, bright eyes because she was crying inside. He looked weary, gaunt, as if he'd lost weight and the loss had been rapid, but, her mouth a tight line, she pushed concern out of sight.

'I wouldn't let that bother you.' She wouldn't be lonely—or only for him. She would have her work and, later, her child. She moved rapidly through the empty room but his voice stopped her before she reached the door.

'You hate me, don't you?'

'Yes!' Her reply was instant, savage, her lips pulled back against her teeth. He confused her emotions, made love and hate seem the same thing, and she could no longer stand the bitter tension. She had to get out of here, find some space, some air to breathe that wasn't tainted with the stench of tension.

Almost stumbling in her haste, she sped from the room and across the large, square landing, taking the stairs quickly, hearing his voice behind her. But for all her haste he reached the foot of the stairs at the same time as she, grasping her shoulders roughly.

'You little fool!' His voice was driven hoarsely through white lips. 'You could have fallen, killed yourself, killed the child!'

Shaken, trembling inside, she returned his angry glare, tugging her arm away from his hurting fingers.

'I would have thought that might have suited you admirably,' she said coldly, nastily. 'Two unwanted encumbrances out of the way in one fell swoop! Why should you care?'

'Of course I damn well care!' he bit, his mouth compressed as he faced her, his hands gripping her shoulders again. 'I care like hell what happens to you and my child!'

Cleo's eyes flicked upwards, searching his. One of them wasn't thinking straight. Either she was hearing things she wanted to hear or he'd made a Freudian slip, admitting paternity in the emotional heat because that was the way he'd wanted it.

His strong hands were still gripping her shoulders, she could feel every fingertip burning through the thin fabric of the sleeveless dress she wore. And he was too close, too male, and too much loved.

'Did I hear what I think I heard?' she asked acidly. She felt his hands drop to his side. 'Do you actually admit the child is yours?'

'Yes.' The admission made his face go hard and she stared at him disbelievingly. Had he finally reached the conclusion that she could be trusted? Had he cared about her enough to work it out for himself? The hope she'd thought was dead stirred to reluctant life again. She was a fool to want him still. He had caused her more pain than she could ever have believed she was capable of handling. Yet love couldn't be turned on and off like a tap, however much one wished it could be.

'I don't blame you for hating me, Cleo, and I have a lot to apologise to you for.' His face was bleak, his teeth biting down on his lower lip as he spread his hands hopelessly in a gesture of defeat she wouldn't have believed him capable of. Then he moved away from her, staring out of the open door to the sunlit tangle of the gardens. 'I don't have the right to expect you to accept my apologies, but I hope you'll believe me when I say I'm desperately sorry—for everything.' He turned then, facing her, his eyes shuttered. 'Under the circumstances I'm willing to give you the divorce you want. It's the least I can do.' A muscle worked spasmodically at the side of his jaw and his voice was husky as he swung on his heels, making for the open door. 'If you want to look around outside while we're here I'll wait for you over there.'

Her mind was reeling. None of this made any kind of sense! He had at last decided he'd been wrong about her, that the child she carried was his—he had even apologised! And yet, he was willing to divorce her! A few days ago, still believing the worst of her, he'd stipulated no divorce for several years!

There was a stone seat against the rosy brick of the high garden wall and he was making for that, to wait for her. All notions of exploring the grounds left her head as she ran after him, her feet slithering on the weedy gravel drive, the full skirts of her summery blue dress flying around her long bare legs.

He heard her rapid footsteps, turned, his eyes puzzled and she told him breathily, 'You can't leave it at that.'

'No?' Whether he deliberately misunderstood her, she couldn't tell, but he went on, 'Don't worry. According to the estate agent, the house is solid. But we'll get surveyors' reports in any case. And as the garden itself is immaterial to me, I'll wait here.' He sank down on the stone seat, his eyes closed wearily—or dismissively—and she snapped,

'I wasn't talking about the house, dammit!'

His eyes flicked open, azure slits. 'If you've got something to say, say it.' He sounded bored and she couldn't understand him, not at all.

'It's about the divorce.' She sat beside him, her heart pattering. She knew she shouldn't hope, but she really couldn't help it. Telling herself that he plainly regarded her as a boring encumbrance, to be offloaded as soon as possible, didn't stop her remembering how he'd said he cared what happened to her and her child.

'It will take time, Cleo, but I'll put the wheels in motion tomorrow.' He spoke gently, as if to an impatient child, and she shook her head abruptly, sending her hair flying about her face. He was obviously determined to misconstrue everything she said!

'I meant,' she began with gritty patience, 'that there doesn't need to be one, surely?'

'What are you? A masochist?' He jerked up from the seat, his body tense with an inner violence she couldn't understand. The line of his mouth was savage. 'It's the only course that makes any sense. When Fiona told me how Fenton had been trying to blackmail you—told me what had really happened——' He smacked one fist into the open palm of the other hand. 'My God! If I see him again, I'll kill him!'

'Fiona told you?' Cleo's mouth was dry. She had thought she could trust Fiona, but the broken promise didn't really signify, not now. She had idiotically believed he'd decided to trust her all on his own, because he cared about her.

'Fiona promised——' she began woodenly, her voice trailing away, and he looked at her, almost sympathetically.

'I know. And yes, she told me. But you obviously don't know her well enough. She always makes her own mind up, and would break a promise with about as much compunction as she would break an egg if she believed good would come of it. You told Fiona what had really been going on between you and Fenton—why didn't you tell me?'

'Oh, God!' Cleo buried her head in her hands, almost laughing but nearer to tears at the injustice of his remark. 'Because you damn well wouldn't listen!' She shot him an angry look. 'Fenton was doing his best to rape me when you walked in that day. And all you could do was jump to nasty, insulting conclusions!'

'I'm sorry!' he groaned, dropping to the seat beside her again, and Cleo, flicking him a sideways look, saw that his hands were shaking. But the spasm was over in a second and he was back in control again, leaning forward, his hands dangling between his knees, loosely held and almost relaxed.

'As I said before, any apologies of mine have to be inadequate and the only thing I can do—after making life intolerable for you—is agree to your request for a divorce.'

She stared at him, wanting to shake him. Of course she had asked for a divorce, but that had been in the heat of the moment, in desperation! Didn't the brute know divorce was the last thing she really wanted? She loved him, she carried his child, he was her husband, for pity's sake! But could she tell him all this, would her pride let her? And could they ever be happy together again? Could they make the marriage work?

She didn't know, but she was willing to try because, somehow, pride didn't come into it any more. And she was turning words over in her mind when he said coolly, 'I shall want access to the child, of course, on a regular basis. You won't make any difficulties over that?'

And then she knew, and the knowledge chilled her, and it was her turn to jerk to her feet,

'Of course I won't.' She pulled herself to her full graceful height, her face ashen. 'Now you have everything you wanted, don't you? A child as an heir, the shares—so what would you want with a wife?'

She twisted on the heels of her strappy sandals and marched away, her back rigidly straight, her emotions heaving. 'I'm going to look over the grounds,' she spat over her shoulder. 'While you sit there and count your blessings!'

She could see it all now. Every last thing had become hideously clear. He had already been thinking of children when she had made that reckless proposal. Not because he particularly liked children, but because he needed an heir. And along she had come—presentable, intelligent, and wealthy in her own right, dangling the Slade shares as bait!

Those shares had been the deciding factor, and now he had them, and he would have the heir he'd wanted— so what possible use could he have for a wife?

Tears were streaming down her cheeks, blinding her, and she stumbled through a thicket of shrubs, not knowing or caring what she was doing, and she heard him call her name.

He was close behind and there was nowhere to go, and she hated herself for the weakness of tears because now he would know.

'Cleo.' A hand held her, another pulled at branches as he extricated her, and then both hands cupped her face, tilting it, the pads of his thumbs wiping the shaming tears. 'Does it matter to you so much?'

'What?' Her mouth was mutinous. Two could play the game of deliberate misunderstandings.

'The divorce. It's what you wanted, after all. And I owe that to you, at least.'

Angrily, she jerked her head from his hands, her eyes flickering, looking for escape. But there was nowhere to go; he was blocking the only way out of the tangle of bushes she'd landed herself in.

'It's what you want,' she denied. 'So why not take it? You already have everything else you wanted—an heir on the way, those shares——'

'Those wretched shares again!' He looked puzzled, as if she'd just told him he'd grown a second head. 'Damn the shares! I'm already in the process of handing them back to you, in any case. I've got enough on my plate without having to contend with that doddery old board of so-called directors, and Luke—sweet heaven preserve me from Luke! It's your baby, your problem, and that's what I've always ever intended. All I ever wanted to do was help you sort the mess out. I thought you might need me.'

Uncomprehendingly, she studied his closed face, shuddering as he added bitterly, 'But you never did need me, did you? Or only as a name on your wedding certificate! And I don't blame you for that, at least you were honest about your reasons for wanting to marry me. I was the one at fault, all the way down the line.' His mouth twisted in self-derision. 'Too wary to insist on knowing why you had to get your hands on your money, too blind to see beyond what my eyes were telling me—that you and Fenton were lovers—and, right at the beginning of it all, too damn smug about my wretched plan of campaign.'

'What plan?' Her brow furrowed and she took a tentative step towards him but he turned away, his face dark with an emotion she couldn't identify as he glanced at his watch.

'It's not important now. Believe me, Cleo, there's nothing more to be said, nothing useful. And it's time we left—if you've seen all you want to see.'

He was walking away, across the shaggy, overgrown lawns and she stared after him, not understanding anything. She felt limp and wretched, her mind in turmoil. He'd said he had never wanted the shares. He'd said so many things that hadn't made sense.

She was used to solving tricky financial problems but she didn't come near to understanding the man who was now striding away from her, not looking back. And she knew that if she let it go now, he would never look back again. He would close his mind on the brief episode of their marriage and she would never begin to understand the enigma who had once been her husband—once, and always, loved.

'Jude!' She ran after him, her feet flying over the grass, and she caught up with him before he reached the car.

'Ready?' he asked, only the slight roughness in his voice betraying any emotion at all.

'No.' She caught his hand, almost sobbing as she recognised the sheet of electifying sensation that engulfed her at the physical contact.

He turned slightly surprised eyes on her, and she saw them cloud, then, as they swept her face, darken with what she might have believed to be torment if she hadn't known better.

She knew she must look a heap, her hair mussed, her face hot and crumpled from crying, from the heat—so far removed from her usual cool and impeccable self that she might be a different person.

'I want to talk to you,' she said, her voice betraying her savaged emotions.

He removed his hand from her curling fingers, which didn't augur well, she thought distractedly, but no matter, she was determined enough and could see, at last, that she had been to self-contained, too afraid of admitting her feelings, too unimaginative to question her own ideas concerning *his* feelings, *his* motivations.

'We've got our lines crossed somewhere,' she told him reasonably. She really did have to stay calm now, quite unemotional, otherwise she would never get the opportunity to know him more deeply, understand why he was as he was.

Ignoring the thunderous bar of threatening brows, denoting a rapid loss of patience, she said, 'You've told me you have no interest in the Slade shares—except on my account. And we both know you married because you want children. And yet——' she took a deep breath, trying to find the right words '—and yet, even though you know I never deceived you with Fenton, that our child will be born in about seven months' time, you are insisting on a divorce. Have I become so repugnant to you? Help me to understand.'

'Can't you leave it alone, woman?' His voice was harsh, the words flying at her bitterly. 'Must you twist the knife in the wound?' His height and breadth, the savage line of his mouth, made him menacing and she moved away from him instinctively, wanting to ease his pain but not knowing how because she didn't know the reason for it. 'Do you want my blood, as well as my peace of mind? I married you because I loved you—I'd been falling in love with you since the moment I first saw you.' The words were torn from him, wrenched out with anguish, and Cleo's heart stopped, then slammed on again and she wanted to go to him, to hold him and love him, but knew that if she touched him he would explode into a savage repudiation of all the hurt and anger he was feeling. She had to allow him to spill out the poison, the pain, she had to stand and watch, and listen, and it wasn't easy.

'And so I hatched my plots, my cunning plans. Emotional involvements between boss and employee don't work, and I wanted our involvement to become very emotional indeed. So I started a rumour. The Mescal Slade takeover of Slade Securities. Very neat!' His mouth curved down with self-condemnation. 'As I saw it, you would hear the rumour and come to me about it. And I would suggest your doing precisely what you are doing—move to your family's company and pull them clear. So far, so good. Their decline was real, as you know, and you were the obvious person to do the job— the best, too. But there was a lot more to it than that, because when you no longer worked for me I could date you, try to make you love me, ask you to marry me. I had it all worked out,' he smiled mirthlessly, 'but before the rumour got to your ears you beat me to it—didn't you just?'

He pushed his hands into the pockets of his jeans, his wide shoulders held straight and proud as he turned away from her, and she held her breath, knowing that she had to stand there, and listen, when one word from her would put things straight. But she couldn't say that word, not yet. He was revealing a side of his character she hadn't known existed, giving her glimpses of vulnerability and self-doubt that made him doubly dear to her.

'Your proposal knocked me senseless,' he said quietly. 'I was being offered, just like that, exactly what I'd hoped and dreamed of having. You—as my wife. And I took the chance, not daring to ask myself exactly why you needed that money because I wanted to hold on to the dream of hope. Hope,' he grated bitterly, 'that I would be able to teach you to love me. It didn't matter why you wanted to marry me, only that you did. Can you understand that, Cleo?'

'Of course I can.' Her voice was ragged, her clear eyes bright with tears of happiness. And he was calmer now, the hurt and anger partly expunged by his bitter, tormented words. 'Jude——' She moved towards him but he shrugged away.

'I don't want your pity. The blame's all mine. I took what I wanted most in the world, and then I spoiled it. I loved you so much that the very thought of you made music in my soul and then, when I was beginning to believe you were growing to love me, I killed all hope of that ever happening. I found you with Fenton and the truth, to me, was what I'd seen. I knew you hadn't married me because you loved me, and there you were, with Fenton, with the money, or some of it, that you'd been forced to marry in order to control, lying around. A sweetener for the lover you couldn't marry because your guardians wouldn't have approved.' His voice deepened. 'If only you'd told me, Cleo, as soon as we were married, exactly why you had to have that money, I would have made damn sure he never came within a mile of you. And if you had,' he gave her a tired, hopeless ghost of a smile, 'I wouldn't have treated you the way I did, killed any hope I ever had of teaching you to love me.'

'I should have done.' She swayed towards him, her face pale, regrets eating her. She could have saved them both so much misery. But he did love her, had loved her all the time, and that was the most wonderful, unbelievable thing in the world.

Unhesitatingly, he cradled her in his arms, concern darkening his eyes, and she murmured, 'I wish I'd told you everything, but I was so afraid of what he threatened to do—not for myself, but because of Uncle John. And

I was ashamed of myself for getting into such a situation in the first place. I didn't want anyone to know, least of all you. It was something I had to sort out for myself.'

'I know. Please don't upset yourself, Cleo.' His voice was infinitely kind, heartbreakingly sad. 'How did he get hold of that hotel receipt? Don't tell me if you don't want to—it's certainly none of my business, and if you were lovers—well, that's not my affair, either.'

'We were never lovers,' she denied, happy, at peace at last, within the circle of his arms. 'He'd asked me to marry him secretly, but I'd turned him down. I'd already recognised my feelings for him for what they were—infatuation. And once that was out of the way I knew I didn't even like him. Anyway——' She dredged her memory. It all seemed so long ago, so unimportant. Everything seemed unimportant when set beside the knowledge that the man she loved so desperately had loved her all the time. She pressed her face closer to the wall of his chest, feeling his warmth, the masculine strength of him, the gentleness...

'Anyway,' she continued quickly, anxious to get this out of the way, lay the ghost of her supposed affair with Fenton finally and for ever. 'He seemed to take my rejection fairly well, said he'd like to keep in touch, that sort of thing, suggested we went for a day in the country—we'd done that whenever I could spare time from my studies—I'd always found it relaxing. So, we went. He was driving my car. We had a picnic lunch, explored a ruined castle we came across, began to make our leisurely way home. But he appeared to lose the way and the upshot was, we were approaching some village— Goldingstan—in the early evening. And there was a bridge, and I never knew how it happened, but he seemed to lose control of the car. It wasn't a bad accident—the left wing was crumpled and I ended up with bruised ribs.'

She shivered slightly at the memory, knowing, now, that it had all been set up, carefully planned. 'By the time he'd walked into the village and found a garage willing to tow the car in for a check, it was too late to do anything but stay where we were. I was feeling a bit groggy by then, and sat in the lounge of the Red Lion while he booked us in, explained what had happened, and ordered supper. It was only when he'd taken me up to the room that I discovered he'd booked us in as man and wife. He said there weren't any other rooms available, and I don't know whether I believed him but I did know I wasn't up to making a fuss, finding the landlady and so on. But I didn't sleep with him. I spent the night in an armchair, and for some reason—the aftermath of the shock of the accident, I suppose—I slept right through until eleven next morning when he woke me and told me that the landlady had been knocking on the door because it was time we vacated it. And that's all there was to it.'

She felt his arms tighten around her, heard him swear, low in his throat, then he murmured, 'It's done with now. You need never worry about him again, I'll see to that.' He released her gently, pushing her upright. 'Are you all right?'

He looked concerned, and she nodded, her heart full, almost hurting with happiness, with her love for him, as she prompted, 'When you read that Fenton was engaged you decided, with him beyond my reach, as you thought, that you'd try to make our marriage work again—but I told you about the baby and you immediately thought——'

'Don't!' he pleaded hoarsely. 'I think I was insane with jealousy by then. And now you know why I'm willing to give you the divorce you asked for. I treated you despicably, and divorce is the only thing I can do for you now.' He shrugged minimally. 'I think we should go now. I've said more then I ever intended to, bared my soul until it's raw. Soul-searching never suited me!'

His wry attempt at humour, to lighten the anguish he was obviously feeling, made her heart contract with love for him, and there was a shaky smile on her lips as she said, very clearly, so that there could be no mistake, 'I don't want a divorce. I never did. I love you, and I need you, and if you won't believe me,' her voice rose to the kind of wailing quiver that would have appalled her in any other circumstances, 'and if you turn your back on me one more time, I'll——'

Words failed her, no threat too dire to utter, but her throat choked up with tears and laughter and utter, utter relief as she saw incredulity replace blankness, and open joy replace that.

'Do you mean that?' He seemed frozen to the ground, making no move towards her, but she did it for him, going to his arms, clinging, holding him, tears not far away, laughter just below the surface, making coherent speech impossible. But his arms enfolded her and the gentle caress of his hands said more than words. And then, with his broken words of love murmured against her lips, her throat, she told him, with the need of all lovers, exactly how and where and when her love for him had begun, and grown, exactly how it was for her, now, and always. And the sun passed its zenith, the lazy heat of the slow afternoon enfolding them as they clung together, as if neither could bear to release the other. Ever.

It was the Thornwoods' evening off, Cleo remembered as she and Jude entered the empty house later that evening, hand in hand. He turned her, catching her in his arms, and she murmured, 'You know, I think I'm hungry. Just let me shower, then I'll fix us something to eat.'

'You shower.' She felt him smile against her lips. 'I'll bring something up to the bedroom to appease your appetite.'

And so he did; himself, champagne and two glasses, which was perfect, and Cleo, already reclining against the satin-covered pillows, fresh from her shower and languid with love for him, told him, 'Lovely, I'm ravenous!' and saw his eyes darken with desire, soften with something that came near to adoration.

His eyes wandered over the drift of amber silk that was her négligé, and he turned away with every appearance of regret, telling her as he stripped off his T-shirt, 'I'll be two minutes under that shower, no more. By the time you've poured the champagne I'll be back.'

And he said, over the noise of the water, 'We'll buy Dene Place, shall we? I've taken a fancy to it. You could say it's where I found you.'

She didn't answer, he wouldn't have heard her if she had. In any case, she didn't need to. They wanted the same things, always would, and they both knew it, now.

And when he came back, the bronze of his skin glistening with a thousand tiny droplets of water, she felt the familiar yet devastating kick of desire in her loins and closed her eyes. Suddenly, stupidly, she felt shy, like a new bride, as if their loving would be for the first time.

'Fiona said,' she uttered thickly, sensing him close, standing over her as she lay back amongst the pillows, 'that you and I didn't have enough gumption between us to figure our way from A to B in the world of the emotions. I think she could have been right.'

'So do I.' His voice was very near now, his clean breath fanning her cheek, and as the mattress depressed beneath his weight and his knowing hands began to remove the silken barrier, working their indescribable magic, he murmured throatily, 'It's a problem we're both going to apply our minds to, aren't we, my darling love? Not to mention our bodies, of course. We'll learn our way from A to B together—and far, far beyond. You and I, my love,' his voice deepened, 'are going to be an unbeatable combination.'

HOW FAR CAN LOVE BE CHALLENGED?

REDWOOD EMPIRE *By Elizabeth Lowell* £2.95
The best-selling author of *'Tell Me No Lies'*, creates a bitter triangle of love and hate amidst the majestic wilderness of America's Northwest empire. 19-year old Maya Charter's marriage to Hale Hawthorne is jeopardized by her lingering feelings for her former lover — his son, Will.

CHERISH THIS MOMENT *By Sandra Canfield* £2.75
Senator Cole Damon is Washington's most eligible bachelor, but his attraction to journalist Tracy Kent is hampered by her shocking past. If their love is to survive, he must first overcome her fear of betrayal.

BEYOND COMPARE *By Risa Kirk* £2.50
When T.V. presenters Dinah Blake and Neil Kerrigan meet to co-host a special programme, the only thing they have in common is their growing attraction for each other. Can they settle their differences, or is their conflict a recipe for disaster?

These three new titles will be out in bookshops from March 1989.

WORLDWIDE

Available from Boots, Martins, John Menzies, W.H. Smith, Woolworths and other paperback stockists.

THREE UNBEATABLE NOVELS FROM
W☻RLDWIDE

STOLEN MOMENTS by Janice Kaiser £2.75

To escape her tragic marriage Lacey Parlett kidnaps her daughter and is forced into hiding. Now, with the FBI closing in, she is desperate to stay anonymous – but one man is dangerously near to discovering her secret.

SARAH by Maura Seger £2.95

The first of three novels in top author Maura Seger's captivating saga on the Calvert family introduces Sarah – a formidable woman torn between the man she loves and a society she hates during the American Civil War.

STRONGER BY FAR by Sandra James £2.50

Kate McAllister's ex-husband has been kidnapped. With less than 48 hours to meet the ransom demands, she has only one option left... one she had sworn never to take!.

These three new titles will be out in bookshops from April 1989.

Available from Boots, Martins, John Menzies, W.H. Smith, Woolworths and other paperback stockists.

UNSTOPPABLE ROMANCE

Folly to Love
LYNN JACOBS

Take Away the Pride
EMMA RICHMOND

A Question of Trust
SHIRLEY KEMP

Designed with Love
KATHRYN ROSS

Mills & Boon are proud to present their 1989 NEW AUTHOR SELECTION

The selection features four brand new novels from some of our latest authors. Varied storylines guarantee a strong mix of love, drama and sparkling entertainment which proves that romance is unstoppable!

Price: £5.00   Published: April 1989

Mills & Boon

Available from Boots, Martins, John Menzies, W.H. Smith, Woolworths and other paperback stockists.